Olabode C

Olabode Ogunlana, B.A.(Hons), M.A., M.B.A. is a Chartered Insurance Practitioner. He was the first Nigerian Managing Director of the National Insurance Corporation of Nigeria. Since his retirement from active insurance work the author has devoted much time to the study of Yoruba Culture and Language.

YORUBA LOVE STORIES

Books of Africa

Publisher: Books of Africa Ltd

16 Overhill Road

East Dulwich

London SE22 0PH

United Kingdom

Website: www.booksofafrica.com

Email: admin@booksofafrica.com

      sales@booksofafrica.com

Copyright © Olabode Ogunlana 2013

ISBN 978-0-9926863-3-8

All rights reserved, no part of this publication may be reproduced, stored in a retrieval system, or transmitted in any form or by any means, electronic, mechanical, photocopying, recording or otherwise, without the written permission of the Publisher, except for brief quotations in printed reviews.

A CIP catalogue record for this book is available from the British Library.

Printed in India by Imprint Digital Ltd.

Books of Africa

YORUBA LOVE STORIES

OLABODE OGUNLANA

Contents

PREFACE

The Yoruba language is exceptionally rich in proverbs, adages and sayings. The stories featured in this book highlight these and at the same time emphasise moral lessons.

In conformity with the definitions of 'stories' and 'tales' given in *A New English Dictionary on Historical Principles,* these stories are composed not only to instruct and amuse, but also to preserve the history of the facts or incidents from which they arose.

OLABODE OGUNLANA

THE FRUIT OF PATIENCE

The attractive little town of Bafe nestles neatly within a cluster of hillocks, and with its sixteen hills, sixteen rivers and streams there had long been speculation that the number sixteen is significant for the community. The old legend arose from the prediction of Adifase, a renowned *babalawo* (diviner, follower and devotee of Orunmila or Ifa, the Yoruba god of wisdom and divination), popularly known as *Baba olomo merindinlogun* (father of sixteen) who lived during the reign of Awujale Obanta. He had foretold that *erindinlogun* (16) would bring Bafe great good fortune in the distant future and this had further heightened the great expectations of successive generations of Bafeans.

Bafe has many orchards. Gunsennodu, an *olubafe* from the old times, planted the first one in between the Ibu and Omidu rivers. Since then many more have been established. Bafe's sheltered climate is ideal for growing fruits such as avocado, orange, mango, banana, pitanga (Brazil cherry), pineapple, different kinds of berries, as well as others not mentioned in this story. Unsurprisingly, Bafe's fruit market is the most popular in the area. Traders and others from nearby towns

11

flock to it. Bafe is also a very popular fishing resort. In addition it boasts of many delightful sites good for camping and picnics. All these natural endowments, enhanced by the hospitality of its inhabitants, have made Bafe a favourite place to visit.

Bafe's strategic location has also helped its development. It is midway between the two most prominent towns in the region; and it is only seven miles away from the headquarters of the three foremost churches in the district. The head of one of them, a white priest, an eloquent speaker who is fluent in Yoruba, attracts many people to the church's services; thus, members of its congregation also visit Bafe regularly for fruit as well as for *afon*, African breadfruit, a food well known for its curative qualities.

One of the best known landmarks in Bafe is Baba Tapa's compound, a cluster of houses at Idera, on the slope of one of the hills to the north of the town. This compound houses not only members of Baba Tapa's family but also his various businesses and residences for his managers and workers. Baba Tapa's main business is rearing a special breed of fleshy, hornless cattle; the locals call them *eranla*. He also raises ducks, guinea fowl, and pigeons.

Baba Tapa has two mills, one for grinding rice and one for corn. His rice farm is the largest in the district. Reports say that he is a good, God-fearing person and a benevolent employer who pays great attention to the welfare of his staff and their families. In those days this was rare and it was highly appreciated, especially as there was poverty among farmers and other people in a rural area such as Bafe. No wonder everyone admires Baba Tapa and sings his praises.

The river Alase flows through his grazing land. On its bank is a pleasant garden and an orchard adjacent to his rice farm. But by far the most valuable and priceless possession Baba Tapa has is his stunningly beautiful daughter, Omodara, popularly known as Dara. Everyone asserts that she is extremely graceful and attractive; they all extol her humility and her charm.

At first, many thought that Baba Tapa was not a native of Bafe but one of the elders in the town who knew him as a child says otherwise. He explains that Alimi (Baba Tapa's given name) is the son of the well-known Omolaja of Mapagha compound. The present site of Baba Tapa's compound used to be Mapagha's farmland. Alimi, a handsome boy in his late teens left Bafe some forty years earlier to study Arabic in Bida and having become a renowned Arabic scholar he moved on to Mokwa. He was fortunate to have as his wife one of the daughters of Sheik Saidu, a Mokwa chieftain and scholar. He was Alimi's tutor, mentor and father-in-law. Alimi's wife was said to be the prettiest girl in Mokwa at that time. Out of the many suitors seeking her hand in marriage, she, with the support of her parents, chose Alimi because of his humility, his learning and fear of God. Omodora, a carbon copy of her mother, is equally beautiful and adorable.

Since Alimi's return to Bafe he has become very attached to the town and he is foremost in his moral and financial support for the development of the town. He is therefore very popular with both the elders and the youth, for whom he is a role model. He sponsors many of the bright young students of the town and the children of his workers at Bafe's leading secondary school. All his employees are said to be extremely loyal and hardworking, no doubt in return for his goodness and generosity.

Understandably, Dara has many suitors. Alimi is extremely wealthy, having previously been a successful merchant in Mokwa. He and his wife want their daughter to marry a good, God-fearing man who will make Dara happy and also be a good son to them; the more so as Dara is their only child. Many of the suitors come bringing costly and rare objects as gifts. These presents are carefully stored away. However, Baba Tapa appears to be in no hurry to give his daughter away in marriage. Eager suitors became disenchanted and frustrated but there was nothing they can do but await Baba Tapa's pleasure.

Dara appears in public only very rarely, except that she occasionally visits the weekly market with her many friends who often visit her at Alimi's place. Bafe market occupies an important place in the life of the town. Apart from the special weekly market there is a daily market which is held in the morning and evening. The market is not just a place for buying and selling: young people meet there, especially at the night market, where the *sakara* music group performs regularly. The latest news from far and near is also exchanged there. The weekly market days in Bafe are like festivals, and many young men from neighbouring towns come to gaze at Dara's beauty, as well as at her pretty companions. One of the old women, a trader in the market once observed: "Everyone flocks to our market not just to buy our farm products but also to feed their eyes, and some perhaps with beating hearts in search of the rare flower," an allusion to Dara.

One market day, Obaleke, the first son of Oba Adeolu and the most eligible bachelor in Bafe, comes to the market with his friends to luxuriate in Dara's beauty. One of them calls attention to Dara's manner of walking: "Look at the way she glides; see her shapely feet as well as her well sculptured figure; some extra time must have been spent in her making." Yet another, pointing towards her, says, "Look how she is smiling at that poor old woman whom she asks to sit beside her - it's unbelievable. Her teeth are like white pebbles on a river bed. Isn't she bewitching? Her simple but elegant *buba* and *iro* with her head-tie stylishly perched on her head like a bird ready to soar into the air make her wonderful to behold." The usually quiet Muse adds: "Her companions are also very beautiful, but she is by far the prettiest of them all."

On this day, Dara and her companions make many purchases and all the porters are vying with each other to carry her baskets.

One of his companions says to Obaleke ,"Why don't you try to woo and win her; she will make a lovely wife." Obaleke merely smiles without making any comment. His silence and inaction appear strange to his companions as it is an open secret that he loves Dara. At last Dara and her friends complete their purchases and are leaving. Quite a crowd follow them. They all watch until the wrought iron gate of Baba Tapa's compound shuts behind them.

Soon after that visit to the market, news spreads that Dara is ill. Everyone anxiously follows the reports of her ailment. Her affliction lingers for some time. Then comes the horrifying news: Dara is dead! The whole town and the entire district are in a state of shock. Everyone is devastated. The mourning that follows is deep and moving. Baba Tapa's compound is besieged by streams of sombre visitors. Condolences pour in from far and near. Three months later Alimi announces that Dara's many suitors are to come and collect their valuable presents. Some come while others do not respond.

After another six weeks Alimi makes yet another announcement. On this occasion only one fails to respond. Rumour is widespread that Obaleke was one of the suitors. Reports also say that Alimi, for reasons best known to himself, had previously but politely refused an approach from the palace on his behalf.

After a long and thorough search, Alimi discovers the identity and whereabouts of the elusive wooer. Alimi then sends for him. The handsome young man, Olorunleke, eventually puts in an appearance. He apologises for the delay in his coming, adding that since the announcement of Dara's death he had been in deep mourning and was in no mood to communicate with the outside world or receive visitors. He had been praying day and night for the repose of Dara's soul. These are his exact words: "From the day I first set eyes on Dara on one of her visits to the market, something tells me that she is my future wife. Although her beauty was stunning, it was her humility in dealing with people that won my heart. The way she talked to all and sundry including the beggars and the market women was indescribable." He adds: "Dara, unlike her friends, did not walk, she floated. The way she interacted with others was remarkable. I remember watching her help a young girl whose basket of oranges fell off her head. That vivid picture showing her spontaneous willingness to help a lowly person has remained in my memory ever since." He gives Baba Tapa, Dara's mother, and other members of the household his deep condolences and prays that God in his mercy will console them. When leaving Alimi asks him to collect his many gifts and presents to Dara. His response is: "They are no longer mine. They were my gifts to Dara. Please dispose of them as you wish and give the proceeds to the poor." In bidding him goodbye Alimi says, "Although Dara has now passed away, we would like to have your friendship. Please visit us from time to time."

Alimi then starts to make enquiries about Leke and his background. He discovers that he is the last son of Oba Ajagbe who had died a few years before then. At the hottest point in the struggle for the appointment of Ajagbe's successor as king, Leke and his mother quietly slipped out of town to a new home where they now live. Here, God had blessed him and he was popular with all his neighbours. Leke, who before all these happenings was single and seemed to be a confirmed bachelor, had heard of Dara's beauty. So he visited Bafe market to see for himself whether or not her beauty had been exaggerated. On the announcement of Dara's death he, like everyone else, was devastated.

Leke has now become a frequent visitor to Baba Tapa's compound. One day Alimi says to him "I want you to assist me in a new venture. Please come tomorrow so we can discuss it." On the following day Alimi invites Leke to inspect the farm where he grows various herbs and trees.

"This is my new venture," he says to Leke. The farm is located at the farthest end of the vast compound, towards the area where the Alase river disappears underground. They go through a low hedge into a pleasant shrubbery. Beyond is a wooded area and an orchard. It is a peaceful place with various kinds of fruit trees. The orchard is unique in that it contains fruits that are not known in the locality, some of them being hybrids. Right in the middle of the orchard is a cottage with stone walls. These are covered with various creeping plants: bougainvillea of various colours, morning glory with delicate shades of purple and honeysuckle in yellow and pink. On its left are different kinds of fruit trees: orange, tangerine, lemon, avocado and pawpaw; they are all ripe and inviting. In the distance is a cluster of plantains and bananas.

Alimi and Leke make their way to the rear of the bungalow where the herb garden is located. Many kinds of sweet smelling scents pervade the area. Several other fruit trees dot the orchard, providing shade. Different varieties of herbs are in neat rows beneath the trees; some are in rockeries, while others spread downwards towards the river bank. They come upon workers who are busy weeding and trimming. One is driving new stakes into the ground. Alimi explains to Leke, "The stakes are for the creeping thyme plants; the gravel mulch is to inhibit weeds, nourish and to enable the thyme to gain a foothold". Leke whispers quietly to himself, "This is a little garden of Eden."

Alimi continues with his explanation pointing out the types of herbs, their properties, the time to plant them, their care and handling, and when to harvest them as well as their uses. "These to the right are for the kitchen. Look at those small spring onions, it is a rare species from Senegal. Those to the left are for medicinal purposes." It all sounds interesting to Leke who becomes really absorbed.

"It's getting hot, let's go in for some rest and refreshment," says Alimi taking Leke's *apeji* (wide-brimmed hat). He places it and his own hat on a table as they go into the bungalow. They enter a room which is cool; two of its ends are open-sided. The one to the left opens onto the garden surrounded by a wrought iron fence crafted in beautiful patterns with a decorative archway. Covering it are many creepers;

their green tendrils entwine around the iron structure and together with their variegated leaves they give the room a striking look.

The wall to the right has a door that leads into the kitchen. As soon as they sit on the wicker chairs Alimi calls, "Rambe, please bring us something cool to drink as well as the fruit I put on the table this morning." A young lady wearing an apron over her *buba* enters with a tray. Leke is still busy admiring the surroundings, but when a soft and melodious voice says, "Good day Sir." He turns round.

In front of Leke is someone who could be Dara's identical twin. Alimi, seeing the puzzled look on Leke's face introduces her: "This is Rambe, Dara's cousin. She now stays with us to console us. Being first cousins they look very much alike." Leke stammers a greeting while still pondering on how two different persons can be so much alike.

"Rambe, please cut one of the fruits so that my young friend can taste it," Alimi asks.

At first, Leke thinks the fruit is grapefruit, but he then observes that it is much bigger with a more yellowish tinge. When cut the juicy part inside looks pink.

"What is this fruit?" he asks.

"The Ministry of Agriculture from which we obtained the seedling calls it shaddock. Its fruits did not ripen until four years after planting," Alimi replies.

"What exactly is shaddock and where does it come from originally? And why haven't I seen it in the market or heard of it before now?" Leke inquires.

"It is a hybrid of grapefruit and orange. I am told it comes originally from an island in the Pacific Ocean. This is the very first time it has been grown in this area, and because of the long gestation period I have given it the name 'fruit of patience'."

After Rambe leaves the room Leke asks: "Baba Tapa, seriously who is that pretty lady; she is the spitting image of Dara".

"Her name is Rambe; as I said she is Dara's first cousin. Do you like her?"

"Very much, if only for being the cousin of Dara she deserves my liking, perhaps more."

"Well, she is the one who will teach you all about herbs; how to grow and tend them."

"With an instructor like Rambe you can be sure that I shall attend regularly and concentrate," remarks Leke.

Alimi calls Rambe back and formally introduces

Leke, stressing that he was one of the suitors of her late cousin.

"He is going to learn all about herbs from you; he is a very patient person and eager to learn. For Dara's sake make sure you teach him all there is to know. I am sure you will be good to him."

"It will give me great delight to teach him all that I know," Rambe replies with an engaging smile.

Leke is mesmerised to see Rambe so close and near. Her bewitching smile reveals two rows of white teeth in between the thin lips; the pert nose, chiselled chin and the dimples on her well rounded cheeks, as well as her hair, braided in Nupe style – all present an enchanting and captivating picture. Leke is dumbstruck. Although he did not have the opportunity to see Dara at such close range, the uncanny likeness between her and Rambe continues to baffle him and linger in his mind.

The Leke who leaves for home that evening, in the frame of mind into which he has been pitched, is both puzzled and elated. From that day on he becomes a regular visitor. Each day he comes to the herb farm with his heart beating fast and butterflies fluttering in his stomach. He takes his lessons very seriously; and so, Leke and Rambe are together for the best part of every day. Dara's mother, Alimi and Rambe become very fond of him. All the other members of the household also like him as he is gentle, courteous and patient.

One evening, just before finishing for the day, Rambe asks: "Leke, do you really like learning about herbs?"

"Of course, you can see that I do. Day by day I like it more and more."

"But do you really like learning all about herbs, or is it because I am the instructor?" Rambe went on.

"For both reasons; I must be honest."

"Do you like me because I look like Dara and remind you of her?" persists Rambe.

Leke responds, "Here, too, I must be honest; initially I liked you for looking like Dara, but as we work together I start to like you more for yourself. Let me confess, I hate going home in the evenings; during the night I long for the morning."

"Thank you for your honest answers and the subtle compliment." A smile flickers on Rambe's face.

"Rambe, what do you find so amusing?"

"It's good to be liked for one's self; and not because one is a substitute for another," Rambe explains, to which Leke responds: "Rambe, you have bewitched me; with your ways and your beauty I cannot but love you. You also have a good and kind heart. Please excuse me for talking like this."

"You do not need to apologise; the feeling is mutual. You too are delightful to know," replies Rambe.

"Rambe, I think you will make a good wife; but do you know that it takes more than beauty to make a good wife?"

"What else does it take?"

"The beauty of the heart is much greater than that of the face; fortunately you have both. You are so kind and caring. You make me feel so much at home. At first, when I behaved clumsily, not understanding the things you explained, you did not laugh at me or make me look foolish,…After some time, with your permission I shall ask Alimi's approval to make you a formal proposal. When I do so I shall also teach you my favourite song."

"I am looking forward eagerly to your proposal," Rambe responds, sweetly, adding,"…and your song."

When Leke leaves for home that evening the two young lovers hold hands and gaze into each other's eyes, blissfully in love.

Nine months pass quickly until, one day, Alimi

comes to the garden and says to Leke: "When you come tomorrow please come in your best robe as I want you to accompany me to see a respected visitor."

So on the following morning Leke appears in his finest robe. He is overwhelmed to see that the entire household is in a festive mood. When he asks, "What is the special occasion?" Alimi merely tells him that the august visitor has decided to come to the house instead, and a reception is taking place in his honour.

"Where is he?" Leke asks. Alimi's response is *"eniti nwon gbe iyawo bo wa ba ki i ga'run"*, which means 'the groom does not need to tip-toe to see the bride'. "Don't be anxious: the visitor will appear in due course."

Dara's mother enters, in her finest ensemble. All the other members of the household, smartly dressed, are already sitting down. Right in front of their chairs are two others, festooned with decorations: Leke is mystified by the festive atmosphere.

While Leke is still wondering, he hears Alimi telling one of the servants, "Please bring Rambe in and tell Gafar we are almost ready." Soon after, Rambe enters, in a simple but exquisite dress; leading her are sixteen pretty young girls. Alimi asks her to occupy one of the two chairs at the front. He then turns to Leke saying,

"My young friend, a few days ago you asked for my approval to your request for Rambe's hand in marriage. You added that for the sake of the late Dara, whom you dearly loved and in whose memory - as well as for Rambe's goodness and beauty - you wished to have her as your wife. Is that still the case?"

Leke is speechless. Before he is able to reply, Alimi, his own mother and some of her friends enter the chamber. Looking from Alimi to Rambe, a bemused Leke asks: "Baba Tapa, am I dreaming?"

At this point, Gafar, the priest, enters and invites Leke saying, "Come and sit here young man; let's get on with it."

Alimi and the entire assemblage burst into hilarious laughter. Dara's mother then intervenes, "Baba Tapa, please speak and relieve Leke of his suspense."

Alimi then takes over.

"I wanted to be sure that Dara married the right man. We were confused when so many suitors started to flock in, the wealthy, the noble, the great and all. I therefore decided to put all the suitors to the test. You, Leke, are the only one who passed the test. You went into deep mourning as if you had lost a wife. You did not want the return of your gifts. I decided to test you further by introducing Rambe to you as Dara's cousin. Both of you have been together these last nine months. Dara's mother and I, and indeed the entire household, watched how the love between both of you grew and developed. Rambe is in fact Dara, and she has confirmed her deep affection for you. You have conquered us all with your character, Leke. Our elders say, *Suru ni baba iwa*. (Patience is the hallmark of character). Anyone with patience will conquer the world; he will inherit the earth. Please continue as you are, humble, approachable, amiable and good to all. Everyone speaks exceedingly well of you. Even the Oba of this town says that you are a better choice for Dara than his own son." He then adds, "That's the trumpet heralding his approach; he is coming to grace this marriage with his royal presence."

Dara's mother, her face a picture of joy, comes dancing forward. Addressing herself to Leke, she says, "You are the only one fit to taste 'the fruit of patience'. May God bless the union between you and Dara."

YOU SWEET ROGUE

Jumoke was widely known, not only in her father's domain, but in the entire district. She was highly educated and as pretty as she was clever and witty. After a convent primary schooling, she went on to complete her secondary studies at a renowned girls' seminary in the city. Soon afterwards, she went to England for her university education. While reading classics she found time to study music and learn about gardening as well. Jumoke as a child and in her early teens was precocious. During her university days she was described as being dashing and daring, which was unusual for a female at that time; she was nevertheless able to take care of herself. As a result, no-one, male or female, could get the better of her. On her return home she became the toast of many eligible bachelors.

Since her parents had moved to the countryside when her father became an *oba* (king), she preferred to spend most of her time there. She had, in any case, always been a child of nature: she loved the forests and the country environment. That she was living away from the city presented no difficulty to her many admirers. They all came calling: the wealthy professionals, the affluent business men, and the politicians. But to everybody's surprise, especially her parents', she refused to make a choice out of all these suitors. She declined to shackle herself in any steady relationship, as she put it.

One day, a handsome and extremely cultured prince came and asked leave of her parents to court her. As the father of the young man was well known and highly respected, the parents gave the prince a warm welcome. But when the prince arrived, Jumoke had gone to a neighbouring town to visit friends. She returned late in the evening just as the prince, who had come all the way from the city, was leaving. His car had just driven out of the compound when he and his driver met Jumoke's car driving in. The prince turned back; and as Jumoke was disappearing up the stairs the mother called her back informing her that a visitor who had waited a long time had returned to see her.

At first, she started making excuses to her mother that she had been out all day and was tired. But her mother was firm with her. She insisted that Jumoke should at least see him and if need be agree another time for the prince to come back. What motivated the *Olori*'s unyielding stance was that the prince appeared to her to be a smart and dashing young man who would be compatible with and acceptable to Jumoke. Reluctantly, Jumoke came back and received the prince, in what she called her music room where she played the piano in the evenings or sometimes listened to her stereo. After a short while, the prince left without Jumoke seeing him off as would be expected. When her mother asked her how the meeting had gone, Jumoke said that he was not her type. "You should at least be courteous and listen to him," remonstrated the mother. With an enigmatic smile, Jumoke replied saying, "*Ohun ti enia ko ba ni i je ki nfi runmu,*" (meaning what one would not like to eat, one should not bother to sniff at).

"What on earth are you looking for in a man?" her mother asked in anger. "He comes from a good and royal family. He is a highly educated professional man." Jumoke countered the *Olori*'s exasperation: "Mother, he is not my idea of the right man."

Suitors continued to visit her, but she showed no interest in any of them, describing one as a "he-goat"; another as having "the look of a man with roving eyes." She made a lot of rude remarks about the men that came calling on her, and her infuriated parents came to the conclusion that she must really hate men.

Soon thereafter an event occurred which would

have far-reaching effects on Jumoke and her family. Her father, a former forestry officer, was also very interested in gardening. He spent a lot of time in the garden and with the gardener whose name was Olu. He had worked for them for over five years and everyone thought that he had become a permanent fixture in the household.

The gardener and another young man, the cook, shared a two bedroom bungalow, separated from the main house by a hedge. Late one evening, the cook reported that the gardener had left home in the morning and not returned. As a result the garden had not been tended or watered; understandably, everyone was worried.

When the gardener still did not show up on the following day *Kabiyesi* arranged for his driver to go to the gardener's home near the city, to see if perhaps he had gone there, but he had not been seen there either. Naturally, everyone both in the Oba's domain and in the city became even more concerned. The *Kabiyesi* and Jumoke, who both loved the garden, were especially disturbed. A report was made to the police; no one answering the description of the gardener had been seen or detained by them. Enquiries at the various hospitals revealed nothing. The search continued locally as well as in the city for some time; but all the efforts proved futile.

About two weeks after the gardener disappeared, a young man, who claimed to be a gardener, came to see *Kabiyesi*. He said that he had heard about the gardener's disappearance and had come to offer his services. It was with a sigh of relief that *Kabiyesi* received him. After examining the young man's references, *Kabiyesi* asked if one of the referees, Mr. Adekunle was the former official of the Forestry Department.

"Yes, *Kabiyesi*, he said that he had worked under you," the young man replied.

"Yes, he did; he must be getting on in years now," *Kabiyesi* remarked.

"Yes, *Kabiyesi*, he is back home in *Idarika*."

"I'll try you for two days; if you are good, the job is yours."

On the first day the new gardener was asked to put the garden in order and trim the hedges. Later, in the evening the gardener invited *Kabiyesi* to inspect his work. He was surprised to see a transformed garden. He was so pleased that he decided to give the new gardener a few more days and then give him formal employment. He was asked to return the next morning.

When *Kabiyesi* looked out of his window early the next morning, he was amazed to see the gardener already at work. In the early evening *Kabiyesi* came out to inspect the garden. He was surprised to see that a new hedge of ixora had been planted to screen off an area on the north side.

"Whatever is that for?" *Kabiyesi* asked.

"I am making a new compost heap which will later be buried in a pit; it will then be covered in black earth. A few weeks after that I shall spread the earth before planting some herbs on it."

"What do you know about herbs?" *Kabiyesi* asked.

"I used to look after the herb garden at the city council nursery. It strikes me that herbs such as thyme, spring onions and garlic will thrive in this soil."

Kabiyesi was impressed with the young man's answers and by the end of that week he had decided to employ him and give him a room in the servants' quarters. A good rapport developed between *Kabiyesi* and the gardener. While inspecting the garden a few days later Kabiyesi asked the gardener his name.

"My name, *Kabiyesi*, is awkward and, to be frank, I am ashamed of it: it is '*Ewunren*[1]'" he whispered. "I suggest, *Kabiyesi,* that you just call me 'gardener'." he added with a mischievous smile. "*Kabiyesi*, it won't be nice and it may be embarrassing to be called that name, especially by *Olori* and the Princess. Please tell everyone to call me gardener; I won't mind."

"If that is what you wish, so be it," *Kabiyesi* agreed.

Within two months the entire compound had been transformed by the quiet and hardworking gardener. New flower beds had been put in place; the previously neglected rose garden took on a new look; colourful creepers had been planted; and a new rockery with ferns and lilies decorated the alcove beneath the ancient looking *Iroko* tree. The whole compound smelled sweet; both *Kabiyesi* and Jumoke were delighted.

The quiet gardener was scarcely ever seen; he kept himself to himself. One day Jumoke was practising on the piano and seemed to be having difficulties with some notes. Suddenly she heard a guitar playing the same tune she was struggling to master; but the guitar was playing the right notes and rhythm. She quietly went out to the front of the house where she saw the guitarist strumming away, unaware that he was being watched. Quietly, she moved closer and discovered

[1] A euphemism for penis.

37

it was the gardener who was playing the guitar. She coughed quietly to attract his attention, and the guitarist spun round to see who was there. On seeing her, the gardener greeted her and was about to leave when Jumoke asked him to stop.

"Where did you learn to play so perfectly?" she asked.

"I went to a music school," replied the young man.

"Please play that tune once again," Jumoke requested.

"The piece is best played if I sit; do you mind if I do so?" the gardener asked.

"Why should I mind?" Jumoke smiled. So the gardener sat and strummed away.

Soon Jumoke joined him, humming at first, then she started to sing in her clear, enchanting voice. When the song ended, Jumoke complimented him.

"You should be a professional musician, not a gardener."

"I enjoy doing both, Princess," the young gardener replied, adding, "It does no harm to combine them. I usually play when I need to take a rest after physical exertion. Excuse me, Princess, I must go back to work now."

His long strides took him behind the tall ixora hedge. Jumoke bent down and examined the guitar; it was a most exquisitely crafted instrument. She wondered to herself how an ordinary gardener could possess such an instrument. Beside the guitar on the pavement was a book, 'Poems by William Wordsworth'. She returned to the music room full of thoughts, wondering what kind of gardener her father had employed. She was also piqued that the gardener did not react more warmly to her compliment.

The following evening the gardener asked the maid to bring four vases so that he could put fresh flowers into them. About an hour later, he returned the four vases with freshly cut flowers beautifully arranged in them. They were left on a table in the front courtyard by the main door.

Later when the *Olori* returned home she could not but notice the eye catching vases. She called the maid to ask where the flowers had come from.

"The gardener must have left them there," the maid said.

"Call him" the *Olori* ordered.

When the gardener entered the *Olori* commented:"These are beautiful flowers; where do they come from?"

"From the flower beds behind the hedge. I planted them especially for cutting so that you can always have beautiful fresh flowers."

"Come and show me the flower beds," the *Olori* asked.

Accompanying the gardener, she walked the full length of the paved pathway before turning to the left into the partly fenced area. Right in front of her were several flower beds in neat rows, a riot of colours. To her observation "These were not here before," he answered, "You are right *Olori*, I planted them about three months ago, soon after I started working here."

"This is incredible; what's behind that lower hedge?" Olori asked, pointing in the direction of the new fence.

"That's the new herb garden."

The *Olori*'s curiosity was aroused; and for the first time since the new gardener started work with them she went round the garden and, escorted by the gardener, she meticulously inspected the entire grounds.

"The lawns are greener; they look like carpets." she remarked.

"*Olori*, I keep working on them; the new sprinklers

which *Kabiyesi* procured at my request have started yielding results."

"Come inside with me" she said.

"*Olori*, please give me two minutes to take off my working boots and wash my hands," the gardener asked politely.

The *Olori* was sitting in a chair when the gardener eventually entered as the maid was putting down the tea tray.

"Sit down, young man." She then poured a cup of tea, turned to the gardener.

"Would you like sugar and milk?"

He was taken aback. "It's very kind of you *Olori*; a little milk, no sugar please."

"I want you to be frank and open with me; why is a young man, well-educated and highly cultured like you working as a gardener? I have been watching you. I became intrigued when my daughter told me the other day that you explained to her how to play an intricate note on the keyboard. She also added that your display on the guitar is that of a maestro; you also read poetry, she told me. You are so detached and aloof. You just don't fit. Tell me why you took this job."

The gardener smiled. "I am enjoying the work; I

love gardening. Music is my hobby and although I am good on the piano, the guitar and xylophone are my favourite instruments. *Olori*, by the time I leave the palace you will have the best garden and lawns in the district."

The *Olori*, highly amused, remarked "You have not answered my question; by the way what's your name?"

"If you do not mind Olori I would rather not tell you my name." The gardener answered. "I am not being rude or disobedient," he added apologetically.

"That's absurd, why?" *Olori* exclaimed.

"You may feel that it is offensive," the gardener replied, averting his eyes.

"Why so, your name is your own," the Olori pressed him.

"It's a bit unusual," is all the young man would say.

"All the same, tell me," Olori insisted.

"*Olori*, you are old enough to be my mother. I'll give you my name only on one condition: the others must not know it. I do not wish to be an object of ridicule."

More intrigued, *Olori* promised she would not divulge the name.

"My name is Potty," the young man said sheepishly.

"Unbelievable! You don't mean potty as in the one

used by children?" asked the *Olori*.

"Exactly, *Olori*. My old nurse told me that when I was small I was fond of my potty; it was always difficult to divest me of it. She then started calling me Potty. After that everyone in the household started using the name. I was told that I did not mind the name; rather I liked it. I grew up with the name and it stuck."

"You must have come from a wealthy family," the Olori remarked. "What went wrong? Your family must have come down in life. What happened?"

"It's a long story, *Olori*, I do not wish to bore you or waste your time," the gardener said. "I must be off to pick up the bag of manure I ordered from the store before five o'clock. I am most grateful of your appreciation of my work and your interest in me. Please respect my wish; keep my ridiculous name to yourself. Shall we say that it is a secret between mother and son?"

The *Olori* was so stunned and she almost did not realise that the gardener had left the room. She continued to wonder about him. There is a mystery about this young man; we'll find out in time, she thought. Out of curiosity the *Olori* would walk round the compound every evening to admire the work of the artistic gardener, as she often referred to him.

Occasionally, she would tease him, when no one was around: "How is Potty today?" she would whisper. "I am fine, *Olori,*" he always replied in good humour.

From time to time the puzzle of the gardener got into the *Olori's* mind. *Kabiyesi* and Jumoke have now become wrapped up in the garden, she thought; could the gardener be responsible for the upsurge in their interest, she wondered. After further inner wrestling she came to the conclusion that if everyone seemed happy with the garden, why should she worry about the mystery man.

One day the *Olori* and Jumoke were in the courtyard. They both started to sniff. One of them remarked that the aroma wafting in the air was unusual.

"The aroma is strange to me; what kind of food can it be?"

"I can't identify it," said the *Olori.*

"That's exactly what I am thinking."

"But who could be cooking? The cook asked for the day off and he isn't back."

"The smell is coming from the direction of the servants' quarters," said Jumoke. "I'll check."

When she peeped into the kitchen the gardener was absorbed in carefully turning down the stove; he was so

44

engrossed that he did not realise that he had company.

"What on earth are you cooking?" He looked up with a start, "It's beans, brown beans with crayfish and onions. I am using my grandmother's recipe."

"Beans!" exclaimed Jumoke. "That's not the smell of beans, although I am not very fond of them."

"It is, Princess. This is a special recipe."

"It has an inviting aroma; may I taste it?"

The gardener obliged and scooped a little bit on the wooden spoon and passed it to her. After tasting it she said, "Are you sure these are beans? It does not taste in the least like the stuff served at the Seminary that was called beans. This, is delicious."

"It will be even better after it has simmered for a while on a low heat," the young man told her.

Jumoke was amazed: "Wonders will never cease; what's it that you don't know or can't do?"

"Am I to understand that you are saying that you like my cooking, Princess?" the gardener inquired.

By way of a reply, Jumoke said, "You really are something. By the way, what's your name?" The gardener smiled.

"What's amusing?" asked Jumoke.

"You won't believe it. My name is Beans. Noticing

the look of surprise on Jumoke's face, the gardener went on, "Beans, that's my name. I got the name as a toddler. I was always bouncing and jumping up and down. As I grew up everyone used to call me Beans. I liked it, it became my name; and it stuck. It sounds ridiculous, but nice; but Princess, please keep it to yourself. I would not like to be laughed at."

Jumoke smiled and said: "I'll keep your little secret on one condition. Whenever I feel like eating these kind of unusual beans and I ask you to prepare them, you will do so." The gardener agreed saying, "Princess, that will be a great pleasure."

Jumoke then asked, "Can you please teach me how to play the guitar?"

"It will be a delight to do so, Princess; but you will need to get yourself a good guitar." Jumoke said that she would search for one.

The conversation between her and the gardener again triggered off Jumoke's urge to unearth the actual person behind this inscrutable, hard-working gardener.

A week after the beans incident, Jumoke asked the maid to call the gardener. She was in the music room when the gardener entered. "I have now got myself a guitar, exactly like yours. When can we start the lessons?"

"Whenever you wish Princess."

"Why not now?"

And so the guitar lessons started. Every evening, after practising on her piano the gardener would come in; they would play guitar together for an hour, sometimes more. Before long Jumoke was able to produce simple tunes on the guitar. Occasionally, they would perform a duet – with one on the guitar and the other on the piano. At times the joint performance would be vocal; yet, at other times, a mixture of instruments and voices. There was no doubt that a good relationship now existed between Jumoke and her tutor.

At times, when coming for the guitar and music sessions, the gardener would also bring a bouquet of freshly cut, sweet-smelling flowers. On such occasions, Jumoke would feel elated; to her this good gesture on the part of the gardener seemed as if he was courting her. Often her eyes would wander over his soft, almost feminine, fingers as he strummed on the guitar.

On such occasions the persistent urge to unearth the real person behind the gardener's façade would

47

become more pressing. Her sighs would become more frequent; her yearning for a suitor like the gardener would be accentuated. She indulged in daydreams. Often she would wonder ... 'What's happening to me?'

If the gardener's visit occurred immediately after such thoughts Jumoke would say teasingly, "How is Mr Beans?"

"Fine Princess, just fine; please keep this pet name to yourself; do not open me to ridicule."

* * *

Kabiyesi had been on a trip. One afternoon, he returned. The household was in a festive mood. The various servants seemed very busy and the general hustle and bustle meant that one did not need to be told that there would be a celebration that night. The gardener had been requested to bring in fresh flowers.

He had just started his evening duties when the Princess came out looking for him. With a sparkle in her eyes she said, "The time has come for you to redeem your promise."

"Which promise?" the gardener asked.

"I am in the mood to eat you tonight," she replied

mischievously.

"What on earth are you talking about, Princess?"

"I want your special beans, Mr Thickhead. It's celebration time tonight."

"But it takes time to prepare, Princess," the gardener protested.

"You promised. Please go about it right away. I shall wait, no matter how long it takes."

Kabiyesi had invited a few guests. They were all drinking and merry but Jumoke's mother observed that her daughter was just picking at her food as if she was not interested in the meal. Her mother leant sideways and asked, "Why aren't you eating?"

"I am waiting for a special dish," Jumoke whispered, adding hesitantly, "You remember the evening I tasted the gardener's beans? I have asked him to prepare some for me. I have a craving for it."

"You and your ludicrous tastes and whims; beans are most unsuitable for eating late at night. Our elders say *Ewa ki i se ounje a jesun fomode* (It is not good to take beans as supper)."

"Mother, you and your ancient customs."

"Don't you know that beans purge?" her mother asked her. "That's why they are not eaten at night."

"Mother, I have made up my mind - that's what I'm going to eat on this special night," Jumoke responded.

"When Kabiyesi and his guests retire to the room upstairs, I am going to enjoy my meal. I don't mind if you have some of it," she added with glee.

With a sigh, her mother declined the offer.

Some time afterwards, Jumoke sat all alone at the table. In front of her was the dish of beans with a special sauce that the gardener had recommended. She had two helpings and enjoyed it tremendously. Then she sat at the keyboard playing a medley of lively tunes; she was in a kind of mood which she herself did not understand. When, eventually, *Kabiyesi* was seeing his guests out, they all stopped to watch and listen to her, in apparent admiration.

At last the household was quiet. Only one room was lighted. The light was showing from Jumoke's room. She was reading a novel – a romance, compelling and juicy, which Beans had given her with a bouquet of flowers a few days before – and she was determined to finish reading it that night. For no reason she started to think of 'Beans'. What a peculiar name, she thought, remembering that he had said that he would disclose his real name when the time is ripe. Out of curiosity,

Jumoke hoped that it would be soon.

There is something about him, she mused: his fingers, so long and sensitive, do not look like those of a gardener. He speaks with a cultured accent. He is so knowledgeable, he has a detached air; sometimes I feel that he towers so much above me. Definitely, there is a mystery about him. If only one of my so-called suitors would be like him; that would be great fun. Fancy the gardener and the Princess, what a pair, what a thought ... she continued to muse.

Just then she thought she heard someone tapping on the French windows that open onto the balcony. There it goes again. She parted the blinds. She could not believe it. This must be a hallucination; it's impossible! I was thinking about him and he seemed to appear all of a sudden.

The 'apparition' smiled and motioned that she should open the French windows. Suddenly, Jumoke felt faint. For a few moments she felt like someone in a trance. How could my thoughts have transported him here? I must be out of my mind, she thought. She looked out again; the apparition was still there, smiling. It looked so real.

As he said nothing she felt certain she was seeing

an apparition. When the gentle tapping sounded again, with trepidation tinged with expectation, she withdrew the bolts, top and bottom. She was transfixed, looking dazed, while the apparition knelt at her feet. Jumoke was completely dumbstruck. She felt like someone dreaming, She thought she heard a voice whispering, "No, my Princess, you are not dreaming." All of a sudden Jumoke's hands, held by those of the apparition became limp. She was falling; she slumped on the bed; she had fainted. The apparition started to fan her slowly and steadily. Then she slowly opened her eyes and moaned, "What kind of dream is this."

"No, my Princess, it's not a dream."

"Who are you? Where do you come from? Am I alive or dead?" The apparition sat on the bed, putting her head on its lap. She kept whispering "What is happening? Where am I?"

"In your room; in the palace. Don't be afraid; just keep calm. You were not meant for any of your previous suitors." There was utter silence. Jumoke shut her eyes; and then appeared to be dozing. After a few minutes she slowly opened her eyes and looked around drowsily. Her lips appeared to be moving, but there was no sound.

Again she looked around, this time, wistfully. She then raised her head with her mouth open, like someone in a coma. Suddenly she became animated. There was a look of fear on her face. "Please don't hurt me. I meant no wrong. I was thinking about a loved one," she whispered.

"Who were you thinking of?"

"Beans, our gardener. In a way you look like him, except that you look more smartly dressed; but you have an aura … if only one can be sure; … no, it cannot be."

"He is the one holding you."

She did not know what to believe. What a strange dream, she thought. She felt like screaming, but she was too listless to do so, perhaps too afraid. On her face was a confused look, maybe more like someone groping in the dark.

With the distressed look on her face the gardener held on to her and started to rock her.

"Do not be afraid. Keep calm," she thought the apparition said.

Suddenly Jumoke turned and clung to the apparition. They embraced. They kissed.

"Please hold me more closely. I do not want to wake

up just yet; this perfect dream is too sweet to be true. Let it continue undisturbed." The gardener responded with a soothing caress.

They kissed again and again. The gardener lifted her in its arms and gently positioned her in the middle of the bed. They both became lost in a haze … utter silence prevailed. After what seemed like an eternity, Jumoke screamed, while the gardener tried to stifle her scream. With a great effort she shook herself free shouting: "*Ewa, Ewa* (Beans, Beans) you have caught me."

Her mother, sleeping in the next room, thought she heard a scream. She turned. There was the scream again, followed by the words "beans, beans". She screamed back, "Didn't I tell you, you don't eat beans at night. Do not wake the entire household."

"Help me mother; help! help! Beans!"

The *Olori* jumped up. As she opened Jumoke's door she thought she saw a figure disappearing by the French windows. Jumoke, with horror in her eyes, pointed towards the windows still yelling *"Ewa Ewa"* (Beans, Beans). She was frightened; indeed terror showed on her face. "He has got me; Beans, Beans", she still kept shouting, with a terrified look. By the time the mother reached the window, Beans had already disappeared.

The *Olori* herself then became hysterical, shouting, "*Kabiyesi*, help, help! Hold him." *Kabiyesi* jumped out from bed, and came into the corridor.

"Hold who?" he asked.

"Potty" said the wife.

"Where on earth will I find one?"

"No, him, Potty, the gardener."

He quickly ran to the front balcony shouting, "Guards, guards, hold Ewunren. Don't let him go."

As the guards were wondering, the gardener flew past. Thinking that he was running after whoever it was *Kabiyesi* wanted held, the guards ran after the gardener. By the time they got on to the road the gardener had turned into a side street. The two came back breathing heavily.

Kabiyesi was standing by the front door with an expectant look on his face. When the two guards returned they said in unison, "We saw nobody except the gardener."

"Never mind," answered *Kabiyesi*, and slammed the door.

As *Olori* was cleaning Jumoke up, the poor girl was shivering; and she kept on moaning.

"Keep him away from me, keep him away from me. At first he was so gentle with me, so compassionate, so tender .... Then when I clung to him he inflicted so much pain on me but ..."

She had a funny kind of smile on her face, with her dishevelled hair and lingering smirk she looked like a mad woman. She continued to shake and to mumble. Startled and shaken *Olori* held on to her and started to rock her. She then put her back on the bed and covered her up, patting her on the forehead. She continued to hold her and rock her until she dozed off. When she started breathing quietly *Olori* tiptoed out of Jumoke's room.

It was nearing noon when both *Kabiyesi* and *Olori* came down. Both were yawning and looked tired.

"How is she?" asked *Kabiyesi*.

"Thank goodness she is now sleeping quietly."

"What really happened?" asked *Kabiyesi*.

"If what I think is true, then we have a problem," said the Olori very quietly.

"What do you mean?" asked *Kabiyesi*.

"Please send for the gardener." said the *Olori* shouting for the maid. The maid came back to say, "He is not in his room." They were still wondering about this when they heard a car driving in.

"Are you expecting guests?" asked the *Olori*.

"No."

Then the messenger entered and announced the *Oludotun*. Both of them got up to meet him.

"What a surprise *Kabiyesi*. To what do we owe the pleasure of this unannounced visit?"

"I am here to apologise for my son's behaviour."

"We have not seen him; what has he done?"

"Yes, you have; your gardener who disappeared in the early hours of the morning."

"Good gracious, don't say that the young man who posed as our gardener is your son."

"The impudent rascal." said Kabiyesi. The *Olori* slumped into a chair.

"How is your daughter?"

"She is still sleeping."

"My dear brother and sister, we shall make amends. I shall bring him to you to be scolded. He is very much in love with Jumoke."

Later in the evening *Kabiyesi Oludotun* with his *Olori* and a handsome young man called at the palace. The young man prostrated himself before both *Kabiyesi* and *Olori*. "Here I will lie until you give me unreserved pardon. I knew no other way to approach your unapproachable and impossible daughter. She drove me mad."

"Get up my son." said the *Kabiyesi*. A contrite *Adegboyega* rose, only to fall again and hold the feet of the *Olori*.

"Please let me call you mother," he whispered.

"Get up my son. Let's us go up and see her."

"Come in," said the soft voice. She lifted her head up from the pillow.

"Mother, that was a horrible nightmare; it left me devastated. I still feel sore. Oh!

I did not realise we had company."

Mother smiled. The man beside the *Olori* spoke: "I am sorry I disturbed your beauty sleep, Princess. I just could not wait."

Jumoke felt that the nightmare had started again. She was about to scream. "Please do not scream. It's me, Beans. I have come to apologise and to plead my case." Then Adegboyega with a pensive face went down on his knees. Like someone dreaming Jumoke said, "That voice sounds familiar, but it cannot be."

"Yes, it is. I am Beans."

Jumoke's face lighted with a smile. The *Olori*, seeing

the joy on Jumoke's face, disappeared quietly. Jumoke jumped up from the bed and with her face beaming with ecstasy, she flew into his arms and sank her head on Adegboyega's chest saying, "You sweet rogue."

PREDESTINED

1) Early Years, Early Love

It is Monday and my first day at St. Peter's School. The previous Friday I had collected my letter of admission that instructed me to go to Standard 5A at eight o'clock. Instead I arrive at a quarter past seven. I find my way to the classroom, sit down and start reading Daniel Defoe's *Robinson Crusoe*. As is my habit, I soon get thoroughly engrossed in it.

"Hello, fine boy; hello, handsome." I hear the last hello sounding as if from afar. I then look up. Standing in front of me is a pretty young girl who must be about my age. I ask if she is talking to me. With a mischievous smile she says, "I guess so, since there are just the two of us here. My name is Wehinmi. You must be the Lagos boy. I saw you coming out of the Headmaster's office last Friday. You are so handsome. You are mine. I shall show them all, right from the beginning."

"What are you talking about? Who are 'them'?" I ask her.

"I am talking about the other girls in Standard 5A. They are a terrible lot. Mope already has a steady boyfriend and she is so crazy about him; there will be no problem there. Anyway, she is much older than us. Joko, although pretty, is dumb; I am not worried about her either. But Celina, although much older, is a great flirt. She will try to entice you if only to put the rest of us off. Felicia, she is a bush girl who does not know right from left.

"But the two I am afraid of," Wehinmi adds, "are the 'terrible Ys' – Yetunde and Yewande; they are pretty all right but they are too clever by half. Besides, they are not able to love anybody but themselves! I am here this early to make sure that I am ahead of them. You are mine, you are my boyfriend."

"Who says so?" I ask the girl.

"I, Wehinmi, say so and I mean it," she responds forcefully. "Don't tell me that you already have a girlfriend."

"Me, I have no time for any such nonsense, let alone girlfriends. I have an entrance examination to prepare for. Besides, I am behind with my book reading; I still have ten novels to read and I do not want to anger my father."

"What are you reading anyway?"

After looking at my book she asks, "Who is Robinson Crusoe?"

"I shall pass the book to you when I finish reading it."

"To make sure you remember, my name is Wehinmi. I live with my parents on Old Barracks Road which is within walking distance."

"I know", I reply, "we, too, live on that road."

"That's good, we shall walk home together after school. It will be like that every day. I shall not allow any of the other girls to get near you. You are my boyfriend. I have chosen you."

"You are a small girl; what do you know about boyfriends?" I ask.

"I admit that I do not know much – you are my very first boyfriend. The big girls have taken all the best boys."

Just then the assembly bell rings, summoning us to all line up on the school field. After assembly prayers we re-enter the classroom block. Wehinmi sits down next to me and during the break she introduces me to the others.

To the girls she says: "Labi is my boyfriend. I don't want anyone of you flirting with him or dancing around him."

Later, after school, Wehinmi and I walk home

together. She never stops talking. In addition to telling me her life story she tells me all about her parents and her younger brother. She discloses her likes and dislikes and asks me a load of questions about myself. I only answer those I feel like answering.

Although she talks too much, I must confess that I rather like her. I wonder if she has cast a spell on me? Saying goodbye, she says, "We shall meet at this junction tomorrow morning at 7". And that becomes our daily routine.

But I do not allow Wehinmi, with all her feminine wiles, to distract me from preparing for the entrance examination. In fact, I become more determined than ever to pass my exams with flying colours. Besides, I already miss Lagos and I am eager to get back there.

One day, Wehinmi asks me to accompany her home after school. As soon as we arrive she shouts excitedly "Mummy, Labi, the Lagos boy, is here." Then a tall lady appears from behind the curtains that divide the room. She is very pretty with a fine complexion. Looking at both of them it occurs to me that when Wehinmi is older they will look like twin sisters.

The lady says with a smile, "Labi, I am so glad to meet you. I know all about you. Wehinmi never stops talking about you. She says you are very clever. She thinks that you will top the class. What have you done to my little girl? You must have cast a spell on her. She has asked me to request you to assist her with her preparations for the entrance exams, especially in English. Is it true that you have read over 30 novels?"

I politely answer as many of these questions as I can. I also promise to assist Wehinmi with her studies. "Have some refreshments," her Mum offers. All the while Wehinmi is dancing round me. Before leaving us, Wehinmi's Mum hugs me and rumples my hair.

In the middle of November a letter from the High School in Lagos arrives. I have the offer of a place the following year. Wehinmi also gets a place but at one of the local girls' schools.

In December, we all go for the holidays. As I stay very near Wehinmi, I still continue to see her. It seems that not only is she very fond of me, but so too is her mother.

Then comes 21 December, the day before I travel to Lagos. Wehinmi insists that I stay all evening with her. As I am about to leave Wehinmi says: "Labi, do not forget that you are mine. Please say that I am yours! Although I am so young, my heart tells me that I shall never belong to anyone else. All I am asking Labi, for now, is for you to tell me. 'Wehinmi, you are mine,' That will make me happy all my life."

Under the circumstances what can I do but agree. I say: "Wehinmi, you are mine and I am yours." She jumps into the air, yelps and hugs me. It is all very emotional. An indescribable sensation passes through my entire body. In all my twelve years, I have never had such a wonderful feeling.

Saying our final goodbye, there are tears in her eyes. "I hope you will write to me" she says. "I know I will write to you," she adds.

I did not set eyes on Wehinmi again for ten years. What's more, I did not recognise her when I eventually did….and she was not able to tell me who she was. It took another six years before we met again.

* * *

During mid-December we moved into our new house at Oko Awo. The house, a bungalow, has two self-contained flats. It has a large portico in the front with a big yard at the back. I have the last bedroom with two windows opening onto the yard. I use my room as bedroom and study, which is useful, for I am studying hard for my A-level exams the following May.

Before getting down to serious studies, I decide to give myself a fortnight's break to enjoy Christmas and the New Year. This break will also allow me to take stock of my six years at the High School, as well as to plan my work for the forthcoming examinations. It will give me time to get ready for a clerical job that I hope to secure at the government offices. The hours of work give me at least four hours for serious studies every day.

We move into the new house before our neighbours. We choose the flat on the right hand side. The other tenants, our neighbours, "Uncle Bayo" and his family arrive in early January. Bayo, is an engineer in his early thirties. He has just returned from Germany where he has been studying and getting work experience. Uncle Bayo has a young cousin, Ade, of about my age. He too works in a government department. The cousin and I become immediate friends from our first meeting. In addition, Uncle Bayo is very companionable, and we all get on very well. Within two months Ade and I have become firm friends. He too is studying for an examination. We study together, sometimes very late into the night.

At weekends we usually just take it easy. Most weekends Uncle Bayo travels home to his village about twenty miles away. His main reason is to see his mother whose health is poor. He usually leaves for the village on Friday evening and returns on Sunday evening. This gives Ade and me lots of freedom over the weekends.

About three months after moving in, Uncle Bayo starts to visit Ibadan quite frequently. Rumour has it that he is courting a young lady he intends to marry. After this had gone on for almost eight months we learn that he and the lady are to become formally engaged. The ceremony will take place in Ibadan where she and her parents live. The wedding will also be in Ibadan four months later. I cannot attend the wedding as the time for my examination is drawing near. Ade who accompanied Uncle Bayo tells us all about the ceremony. "It was a grand affair," he says, "and the bride is so pretty."

The newly-weds went to the north for their two week honeymoon. Another two week's stay at Uncle Bayo's village followed. This was to enable the bride, Eunice, and Uncle Bayo's mother, who could not attend the wedding due to her ill health, to get to know each other. The new couple finally arrive in Lagos about four weeks after the wedding.

The bride was as beautiful as Ade had said she was, and very witty. Everyone within the compound, as well as her other neighbours, grow to be fond of Eunice.

Uncle Bayo formally introduced Eunice at a drinks party, to which all the neighbours, including myself, were invited. When we shook hands I could sense a mischievous twinkle in her eye. Was it my imagination? She also winked at me. I feel there is something familiar about her. I seem to have seen her, or someone like her, before. Eunice says that it is her first time in Lagos and she seems to like it. I conclude that, if indeed it is her first time in Lagos, I could not have met her before. Perhaps it was someone with a slight resemblance, I think to myself.

Uncle Bayo and his wife Eunice go out a lot in the evenings during the week. Some weekends the couple travel to the village to see Uncle Bayo's mother. On other weekends, Uncle Bayo goes alone and two of Eunice's girlfriends come to visit. Ade is always there to keep them company.

One particular weekend Uncle Bayo had gone off to visit his mother but Eunice's two girlfriends did not visit. On the Saturday night after studying until around midnight, I become so sleepy I actually doze off. Something awakens me, and I decide to walk around the yard to stretch my legs to help myself stay awake. I had been walking for a short while when I heard Ade and Eunice talking. For some reason, I decide to move nearer to the window, although not really wanting to eavesdrop. However, I distinctly hear Ade's and Eunice's voices.

Eunice was saying: "I find the whole arrangement rather distasteful; I don't think I want to go through with it; the truth is that I have changed my mind; I can also see that you are as unhappy with the arrangement as I am."

"You are right there," Ade replied. "My fiancée is getting worried."

"Why don't we tell him that we are working on it?"

"But one day, he will surely find out that we have not been doing so," was Ade's answer.

"Let's leave it at that for now," Eunice says.

"Good night" says Ade; and the lights go out.

The following morning was a bright Sunday. Ade came to my room just as I was getting ready to have some rest after working all night. "Good morning Fola, or shall I say good night." he says. "The latter would probably be more appropriate."

"There was a particular exercise I had to crack and as a result I did not sleep," I began to explain. Then Ade asked me if I had seen anything of Eunice that morning, commenting that she seemed to have disappeared. "She cannot have gone far. She will show up soon," I remarked. I then pull the covers over my head, as if to signal I really did need to get some sleep.

At about noon I wake up and go into the yard for my usual morning exercise. Ade is sitting on a stool with a frown on his face. "What's the problem?" I enquire. "Eunice is yet to show up. It's strange; she has never gone out on her own before. I always accompany her whenever she is going out," Ade tells me.

"You don't have to worry; she will be back soon; after all she is an adult," I say.

After lunch, I decide to take a stroll. Returning that evening I find Ade on the portico looking around anxiously. "She has disappeared into thin air. I am scared. It is so strange – she has never gone out on her own before."

While Ade and I are still discussing Eunice's disappearance, Uncle Bayo drives into the yard. He is naturally disturbed when he learns that Eunice has been missing since early morning. We then sit down to discuss how to search for her. The most logical beginning for the search, we agree, is to go to the houses of her two friends. Ade did so immediately. First thing the following day, Uncle Bayo decides that, if necessary, he will go to Ibadan to continue the search. Not until then shall we inform the police.

Eunice has not been seen by her two friends and so Uncle Bayo sets out for Ibadan the next day. She had not been seen there either. To be absolutely certain, Uncle Bayo called at their village on his way back. No one there has seen her either. When we check, we discover that none of her belongings are missing. All her dresses, bags, shoes, and jewellery are still in her room. Everyone agrees that this is most strange. A thorough search of her room does not yield any other clues. The report to the police also has no result. The compound, indeed the neighbourhood as a whole, shares our concern. It is quite a mystery. The neighbourhood is rife with all sorts of rumours, speculations and theories. Uncle Bayo becomes increasingly worried.

After a year of fruitless effort, the hunt to find Eunice is called off. Although the search has been abandoned, I cannot stop thinking about her. One night, unable to sleep, I again recall that evening when Uncle Bayo introduced her to me – in particular, that mischievous twinkle in her eye when she winked at me. The strange feeling that we had met before still lingered with me, but I questioned how that could be since it was her first visit to Lagos.

I had already dreamt about her twice. Sometimes strange images of her intruded into my thoughts. Is Eunice a real person? Is she from the spirit world? Why does she leave without taking any of her belongings? What a puzzle!

2) London, Phyllis and The Intervening Years

One day a letter arrives for me. It reads:

"My dear lost friend.

At first I thought I had lost you for all times. When suddenly you reappeared in my life I felt new life surging into me. Then came that evening. At first, I just saw your silhouette but when for some minutes you remained still outside the window I was sure that you were listening to everything we were saying. I was moved. I felt that I had betrayed you. That night I changed my mind. There was nothing else I could do but leave. I did not wish to commit

any indiscretion. Whatever it was you saw or heard was not what you thought.

Something tells me that I shall still have the opportunity to explain everything to you. Since our first meeting you had always been with me. Whether I was awake or asleep, you were always there. It will always be so since you are mine and I am yours. My word is my bond and I would like to think that you think the same.

Sometimes I thought you did not recognise me. I am almost certain that I was correct, especially as you did not show any sign of recognition. There was a night I was arguing with myself. I consoled myself with the thought that you were just being a gentleman and did not wish to compromise me. Your thoughts will always be in my mind. Please be patient and wait for me. I am yours and yours only. It's me."

I read and reread the letter. It did not make sense

to me. Am I reading someone else's letter? I asked myself. But it was clearly addressed to me. Who could the writer be? Why is she writing, as it seems then, in riddles? What am I supposed to do, especially as she does not give me her return address.

Although the letter is not sad, I feel that the writer is in a state of doubt and distress. What should I do? I asked myself again and again. I read the letter several more times thinking that reading it more carefully will give a clue to the writer and why is it not signed. But one night something compels me to read the letter again and a part of it strikes me as strange. It was the part that read:

"Then came that evening. When for some minutes you remained still outside the window I was sure that you were listening to everything we were saying. I was moved. I felt that I had betrayed you. That night I changed my mind. There was nothing else I could do but leave. I did not wish to commit any indiscretion. Whatever it was you saw or heard was not what you thought."

One sentence keeps recurring in my memory – *"I felt that I had betrayed you."* One other point that struck a chord is when she writes, *"I am yours and you are mine!"*

I remembered having heard something similar before.

For the first time it occurs to me that Eunice and Wehinmi might be one and the same person. Eunice and Wehinmi's mother were very much alike, but how could it be she married Uncle Bayo? Here is another puzzle. Wehinmi's face started to haunt me. If I was right, what had happened to her? How was I to find out?

After passing my A levels, I concentrate on saving the best part of my earnings for two years. For this reason I had resigned my civil service appointment to join a commercial enterprise. The pay was much better and merit was given recognition. So I started planning my studies abroad.

I eventually achieve that aim. By the time I travel from Lagos, I have already enough savings to pay my tuition fees for the three years. The night before my departure, I have the feeling that I am not alone. Or perhaps I had been dreaming. But I did feel that I was conversing with the writer of the strange letter.

She kept on reminding me that *"we had plighted our troth; do not break your promise. I have not broken mine, although it might appear to be so. My explanations will more than satisfy you when we meet in due course, as we shall. I wish you a pleasant journey and a safe return. I am waiting to receive your embraces."*

It felt so real that from time to time I peer into the dark corners of the room. I am no longer in any doubt that the mystery letter is from Wehinmi. That night my sleep is sound and peaceful. I awake feeling fresh and alive, and on my flight from Lagos to London thoughts of Wehinmi filled my head.

I arrive safely in London, but my temptations start from my very first day. Our group reach the British Council hostel that morning. One student who is returning for a post-graduate course suggests that we accompany him to the Methodist International House where we find a table tennis tournament taking place. I sit there, seemingly watching the game, but my mind is in another place completely.

Unknown to me, I am being watched. Suddenly I feel a gentle nudge; I turned to my right and my eyes met hers. She says, "Hello handsome, a penny for your thoughts." I say hello. "While you are not exactly bored like me I see that your mind is not on the game. Come on, let's go for a walk."

We walk along Inverness Terrace until we reach the Bayswater Road. We cross over into the park and sit down underneath a tree.

"My name is Phyllis. I am a law student from Kingston, Jamaica. For the first time in the six months I've been here I feel homesick. I miss Frank, my boyfriend. Tell me about yourself," she asks me.

"I am Labi. I arrived only this morning from Nigeria. I am not exactly homesick but I'm missing an old friend terribly. I had not seen her for ten years; and when I did, I did not recognise her. A letter she sent jogged my memory and a few other things that have happened have left me confused. I cannot describe my feelings. I feel so sad and sorry. I wonder what I should do."

"Never mind" Phyllis reassures me. "It appears that we are in the same predicament. Let us be friends so that we can console each other. I shall be your source of strength and you shall be mine."

"That's very kind of you," I replied. "I am sure that we can be good friends, provided we do not get carried away." That is how Phyllis and I come to be good friends. In due course, she becomes like a sister to me. But for her my life and my problems could have become much more complicated.

She shielded me from other would-be girlfriends and London's host of husband hunters. Often, to ward off embarrassment, I introduce her as my girlfriend or fiancée as the occasion demanded.

My stay in Britain is fruitful. Throughout the time, my companion and adviser Phyllis is always by my side. Without her I could not have achieved the success I did. When I get my final year results, Phyllis receives the news with mixed emotions.

That evening she says: "My brother achieved an upper second in economics, so I should feel happier than I am now; but I'm not. The thought that you will be on your way to Nigeria shortly has made me feel very sad – but congratulations again and I wish you more successes in the future".

The following day there is a new development. Frank, Phyllis's boyfriend, telephones to say that he will arrive ten days before my return to Nigeria. I have never seen Phyllis so happy and radiant. It was a great consolation for me that Phyllis would have her boyfriend and would not be lonely.

Days later I board the cargo boat for Lagos. The fortnight on the boat goes by quickly. I make new friends on the ship, one being Maxwell, a newly qualified pharmacist from Eku in the mid-west region of Nigeria. We enjoy our short stopovers in Las Palmas, Freetown and Takoradi.

I need only a week's break before starting my new job as a manager with a trading company that has a large Nigerian network. My posting is to the Head Office to take charge of the western and mid-western regions. My first tour is to Ibadan, the company's Area Office for the west region.

On my first night I find the way to Wehinmi's house at Old Barracks Road. Her parents are still living there, but were away. I leave a note for Wehinmi's mother in which I ask her to remember me to Wehinmi.

On my first tour to the mid-west region I visit Benin City, Sapele and Warri. My main mission is to meet the company's distributors and to get to know the area. One afternoon I take time off to visit Maxwell, the pharmacist who had returned to Nigeria with me. He is glad to see me in Eku where he had just completed furnishing his new store and showroom.

I had mentioned to him that I needed to buy some good fabric and head-ties and asked his advice as to the best store in Warri for such goods. He gives me a note for his young relation. After my business rounds the following day I go to the shop. As I enter the shop, a lady is coming out. I could not believe my eyes – it is Eunice, the missing bride. We both stand still. I speak first. "Is that you, Eunice?" She clasps me with both hands, crying and laughing at the same time. Then she lets me go and pushes me backwards to take another good look at me.

"Is it Fola or a ghost?" she exclaims. "Yes, it's me, dear Eunice, but you have a lot of explaining to do! Let's go inside first," I stammer. As I sit down she pats me on the cheeks.

"Fola it is so good to see you," she says. "You look so dazed and puzzled. I shall explain everything, but all in good time. I am on my way home. Let's have something to drink before we go home. We can then talk in a relaxed atmosphere free from interruption."

As she walks, I cannot stop looking at her. She is a spitting image of Wehinmi's mother, so much so that I have no doubt that she is Wehinmi. She is even more beautiful than when I last saw her. It is a short drive from the shop to her house.

"A good meal before we talk or we talk before the meal?" she asks me.

"I would rather have the talk first. I need answers to so many questions," I reply.

* * *

3) Wehinmi's Mystery is Explained

"Would you mind if I tell my story from the beginning, that way there will be fewer questions to ask. Agreed?"

"Agreed." I answered.

"Eunice and Wehinmi are one and the same person: you need not puzzle your head over that. My maternal grandmother, who, by the way, wants to meet you, named me Temisan Orisewehinmi. My paternal grandfather named me Omolara and at my baptism I was given the name Eunice. I understand that this was my mother's idea, so my mother prefers to call me Eunice. My mother and Uncle Bayo's mother were classmates at the Women Teacher's Training College at Ibadan when they were young. The friendship continues to this day, despite the rupture caused by my disappearance in Lagos. But we shall get to that in due course.

"For quite some time," Eunice continues, "my mother was pressing that I should get married. I always told her that the only person I had ever loved, and would ever love, was my Labi. My mother would always reply, 'But where is your Labi? He never writes to you. You do not even know if he is still alive'.

"One day mummy said, 'I am expecting a visitor tomorrow. He has just arrived from Germany'. 'Who is he?' I asked. 'What was he doing in Germany?' Mother told me his name was Bayo and he was the first child of an old school friend, Oluyemi. 'But why is he coming here, mum?' I asked. 'You will see when he gets here'.

"The next day, just before noon, an impressive sports car pulled up in front of our house. Out came this tall handsome man. As I was at the front door he came straight to me. 'Good-day, young lady. Is this the house of Mr and Mrs Ede?' When I said it was, he announced that he was expected.

"I led him in and called out for mummy. When mum arrived, the handsome man bowed before they both shook hands. 'You have become a handsome young man. Why aren't you married?' mummy asked. 'I am still searching for the right partner,' answered the visitor. 'Please forgive me,' mum said. 'I get carried away. Please sit down and make yourself comfortable. Bayo, please may I introduce you to my daughter, Eunice.' Turning to me mum explained, 'This is Bayo, the son of my old friend and classmate. Eunice, please get our visitor a drink. Why don't we try the lemonade you have just made?'

"Mum and I went into the kitchen. Mum had a knowing look on her face. I pretended not to notice it. I placed the tray with the jug of lemonade and three glasses on the table and asked to be excused. I sat on a chair in my room pretending to be reading. Then mum entered and said, 'Eunice what does this mean? You have left our guest unattended.'

"Mum, don't you mean your guest. Why should I attend to him? He is here to see you," I replied. 'Eunice, do not be difficult. You know he is here to see you. Yemi and I thought that if both of you meet and grew fond of each other you might get married.'

"'So my Mum is now a matchmaker,' I answered, adding quickly, 'Mum, you know that I already have a man of my own. Besides, two persons don't get married just because they are fond of each other. All the same let us go down and entertain the visitor.'

"Dad was away so just the three of us sat down for lunch. Having eaten, and as quickly as it was polite to do so, Mum excused herself and I was left alone with Bayo. I must say that he impressed me as a charming person with perfect manners – and he fascinated me. He disclosed that his mother had been pressurising him to get married. It was she who suggested that he should pay this visit as something might come of it. 'She told me how beautiful and intelligent you are,' Bayo disclosed, 'and so here I am. All I want for a start is friendship and assurance that we can meet again from time to time. Who knows, it might lead to something.'

"I answered that while I saw nothing wrong with this idea, I felt I had to point out that there could be a problem. I then told him of the understanding that you and I had while we were young. He dismissed it with a wave of the hand. 'How do you think that such a promise between two twelve-year-old kids could be taken seriously?' he queried.

"I replied that in our own case, it was a special and binding agreement. When he asked where the young man was now, I answered truthfully that I did not know. 'Yet you are still hoping that he remembers you and the promise,' he said with sarcasm.

"Uncle Bayo took to visiting us almost every weekend after our first meeting, often bringing me presents. I honestly became fond of him. Polished men were rare in our area in those days, and he fascinated me. All my friends thought I was very fortunate to have such a suitor. Then one day he sent me a letter informing me that he intended to visit me the next weekend to ask me for a special favour.

"The letter was brought by Ade, a young man who must have been about my age who looked very much like Uncle Bayo. He explained that they were first cousins. He added that many people thought they are brothers. I asked Ade to tell Uncle Bayo that he was welcome to come.

"He arrived on Friday evening. This time he stayed at a small hotel near our home. The hotel had a night-club with the best band in town. He invited me to join him there the following day, a Saturday, and I agreed.

"Just before he took me home he asked how I felt about our relationship. I told him that I felt that it was fine. He pressed me further and asked if it was a positive enough relationship for us to get engaged. I reminded him that he was yet to make a formal proposal. I add that even after that we would need to wait for at least another three months before getting engaged. I set the three month's limit because intuition told me that I might see or hear from you within that time. He agreed rather reluctantly, on the condition that on weekends when he was unable to come, due to visits to his ill mother, Ade could come to keep me company.

"While agreeing I thought to myself that he wanted to install someone to keep an eye on me. The truth was that I enjoyed Ade's company, perhaps even more than Uncle Bayo's in some ways, because Ade and I are about the same age.

"On getting home I find Mum had sat up for me. She asked how the evening had gone. I told her that I enjoyed it as Uncle Bayo is a very good dancer. Mum wanted to know what else happened. My guess was that Uncle Bayo had already hinted to her that he was going to propose. Mum was disappointed, as I had nothing else to add.

"As agreed, Ade come every other weekend. Like me, Ade is a scrabble fan and good at chess. We, therefore, spent quite a lot of time playing both games.

I got to like him more and more. One evening Ade asked me a curious question. He asked me how happy I should be if Uncle Bayo decided to withdraw his suit leaving the coast clear for him. All I said was, 'What a thought!'. I was to recall that incident afterwards.

"Time flew by and with only two weeks out of the three months I had requested from Uncle Bayo left, there was still no news of you. In the meantime my Mum and Bayo's mother started to make preparations for the engagement. Precisely three months following our discussion I got engaged to Uncle Bayo.

"The wedding was fixed for a month after that. On the night of our engagement I asked Uncle B, as I now address him, why he wanted to marry me when he knew full well that my heart was with someone else. He said that he was willing to take the chance. I again stressed that he would be having a body without a heart. He added that he was sure that he would soon sweep me off my feet. It was the most curious engagement that I ever heard of. I thought I was in a dream.

"We had previously agreed that we would go up North for the honeymoon. Uncle B assured me that I would love Jos, Vom, Bukuru and the other towns and places in the region. Then another curious thing occurred. 'How would you like it if I were to give you another three months of grace after the wedding, just in case your Labi turns up after all?' asked Uncle B. I was astounded and asked him what sort of joke that was meant to be. He said he thought it best that we wait for three months to consummate our marriage.

"I looked at him askance believing he must be joking. But no, he was not. Rather he was paving the way for a favour that he wanted, a favour that he was only prepared to ask, he said, the night before our wedding. 'It can be your wedding gift to me,' he said. Instinct told me that he was serious.

"On the evening before the wedding, Uncle B came to the house and we had supper with my parents. Afterwards, he suggested that we take a stroll in the garden as he was ready to ask for his special favour. We took our wine glasses and another bottle. Sitting down underneath a tree I told Uncle B that I was eagerly awaiting his request. Let me say it almost in his words. He said, 'The doctor told my mother that she had between eighteen months and two years to live. She then asked me earnestly to make it possible for her to see a grandchild before she passed away. As I know that I could not gratify that wish, I was in a quandary.'

I wanted to interrupt him but he asked to be allowed to finish.

"Continuing with his explanation, he told me: 'While in Germany, my favourite sport was polo. One evening I fell from my horse after a collision with an opponent. It was a very bad fall. I was rushed to the hospital. I had an operation the following day. Before being discharged, the surgeon advised me that my chances of being able to father a child were remote. Of course, I could not tell my mother about this when I got back to Nigeria. When the pressure started about my getting married I began to think about what I could do. It was then that I decided that I would take Ade into my confidence. He was the only person I could tell as I have no brother. I then requested him to help me father just one child provided you would agree. He was horrified. He then raised a very important issue. He said that one day he too would get married. He already had a girlfriend he intended to marry. Supposing he was willing to gratify mine and my mother's request, what sort of explanations could he give to a future wife? We also wondered what your reactions would be. The plan was to confide in your Mum after the baby arrived.

"'If you decide against this arrangement, the marriage will still have to take place. A divorce can then be arranged discreetly after a decent lapse of time, and that will leave you free for your lover boy. What do you say?' I was so flabbergasted by the strange request I could not speak. I had to think fast. After walking around in the garden, I came to a decision. Having logically marshalled my thoughts, I decided that calling the marriage off was not a possibility – the shame would kill my parents. I would talk to Ade. Both of us might agree to go along with this scheme, but there was no way I could sleep with him - or anybody else for that matter.

"But I knew that I could share my bed with Labi, for my spirit was telling me that he was still alive and he would find me soon. Besides, this was a way for me to buy some more time to find him. I was sure that Ade would go along with me.

"I walked back to where I had left Uncle B and told him that the marriage would go ahead. He hugged me and said that God would bless me. Just getting married, he said, would calm his mother down. So we walked back to the house hand-in-hand. Uncle B said good night to my parents and went to his hotel.

"The wedding took place. We enjoyed our stay in the North, wining, dining and dancing each evening.

When we arrived at Uncle Bayo's village, my mother-in-law was so happy. It was as if her grandchild had already arrived. But my trouble started when we got to Lagos. I could not believe it when I saw you; but you did not recognise me. To compound my problem, when I asked Ade your name he said Fola. I just could not figure it out. That night I could not sleep, as my mind was racing so fast.

"I tried to see you alone so that I could speak to you, but there was no chance. For two days I was ill. I was depressed and restless. What could I do? Then it occurred to me that I would ask Ade your full name. When I asked him and he said it was Afolabi, I had such a sense of relief. Unfortunately it was on that evening that I decided to tell Ade to call the whole plan off. That was when I saw you outside our window. I was frightened that you would have heard our conversation and you would have jumped to the wrong conclusions. Ade and I had never been romantically involved. He was in love with Yeside, his fiancée. He was so relieved when I told him to abandon the plan. But I did not tell him about our previous relationship.

"During the night I thought it through. I would leave first thing in the morning while all of you were still sleeping. I would go into hiding. When all the hue and cry had died down I would make contact with you. I had never been so happy in my life. To think that it was Uncle B who brought about our reunion. I knew too that Uncle Bayo would have no objection to us obtaining a divorce. Although I was only a twelve-year-old when I first set eyes on you, I truly fell in love with you. You would not have believed what I was thinking when I saw you leaving the Headmaster's office. Something told me this was my future husband.

"Do you recall the last evening we spent together before you left for Lagos? I almost died of grief. Throughout Christmas and New Year I was ill. I could not tell Mum what the matter was. When all the other girls started bringing their boyfriends, Mum would ask for mine. I always reminded her that she had met and liked you. I assured her that God intended us for each other and it was meant to be. I am not sure that she believed me."

At that point I interrupted her to ask: "When you ran away from Lagos where were you hiding so you could not be found." She asked if I remembered Felicia, our classmate. It was to her she went because no one would think of looking for her there. "Instead of my afro cut I grew my hair and started to plait it. I started accompanying Felicia to Warri and Ashaka were we bought fine materials for sale in Igbara Oke. We would travel all over Ekiti – Ado, Iyin, Aiyedun, Efon…"

Continuing her narrative, Eunice (or should I now call her Wehinmi?), told me: "After one year when the hue and cry had died down I registered at the Polytechnic to study for a degree in Social Science. At the same time Felicia's mother was teaching us how to sew. I eventually ended up in Eku with Daddy's cousin, Maxwell's mother.

She gave me a small shop in Eku. After two years I had saved enough to rent a shop in Warri. I deliberately continued to use my married name to ward off the wolves. I told them that my husband was away in the UK studying. The shop grew. I took the adjoining one and then a third one. I became the largest distributor of George materials and Hayes head-ties. I started doing wholesale business.

"One day on a trip to Benin City I ran into Ronke, our next door neighbour in Lagos. It was she that told me you were away in Britain studying Economics. I begged her not to tell anyone that she had seen me. We became good friends and I gave her goods on credit.

She was creditworthy and paid promptly; in addition she kept my secret.

"Before you go on with your questions I have some of my own, otherwise I shall die of anxiety. I hope you have not entangled yourself with any lady? I hope your love for me has grown as mine has. I have never loved anyone else. I knew you were mine because I said it. I bewitched you. More accurately, our union was predestined."

All the time she had been speaking I never stop looking at Wehinmi. When I indicate that I want to say my piece she suggests that we should first take our meal as it was getting late. Before that, however, she embraces me and gives me a kiss, with fervour. The way the kiss was returned assures her that my long wait had not been in vain.

After the meal I tell my story, especially about the stay in London, full of praise and gratitude for Phyllis whom God had sent to assist me. I say that as soon as Wehinmi can obtain a divorce we would get married. At her suggestion we agree that the honeymoon would be in Jos. She reminds him that her grandmother would like to see me. As she lives in Warri we agreed to visit her the next day.

4) A Wise Granny and a Blessed Union

It is mid-morning when we arrive at Granny's compound, and we greet about a dozen relatives before we get to Granny's apartment. As we enter, there she is: a dignified, elegant, old lady. Her white hair had been brushed back tightly on her head and, despite being in her nineties, she is still an attractive woman. She exudes a lively aura and her pretty eyes still sparkle brightly. There can be no doubt of where Wehinmi and her mother take their beauty from.

She greets us very warmly and Wehinmi presents me to the old lady. "Labi, this is Gran. She was looking forward to meeting you. She was the only one who believed that you were real, alive and would come back to me. She was always speaking about you, especially after she had read my palms. She said that I would be eternally indebted to a lady who would save you for me. She went on to say that the woman was someone with honour; and though greatly attracted to you her conscience would not allow her to come between you and the woman you loved."

"Welcome, my son. I knew that you would come one day," Gran said. "Often I saw you in my dreams and visions. I took to you from the first time I saw you.

I was told that you were Wehinmi's husband. I was assured that it was meant to be."

"Gran", I replied, "Wehinmi and I were about twelve years old when we first met. How could she know at such a tender age that she was in love with me and I with her?"

The old woman answered my question with these words. "My son, there are many things that men do not understand. Although you and Wehinmi were biologically the same age, she was more mature than you. The creator ensures that girls mature far more quickly than boys. When you met you were twelve. Wehinmi had the maturity of a girl of about sixteen. Besides, like me, she is psychic and has the 'gift'. It must have been revealed to her that you were her husband to be. When her mother became worried that she was not interested in boys, I tried to assure her. I told my daughter that Wehinmi had already given her heart, her life and all, to someone who was predestined for her. Wehinmi's mother did not believe me, but I was convinced, and even more so when one day I read Wehinmi's palms when she was here on holiday. There it was clearly written that Labi was to be her husband. Although it was indicated that several years and many

miles would separate you both, it had been ordained. "I also saw that both a woman and a man would threaten to come between the two of you; yet you would both overcome all impediments and eventually share the life that had been mapped out for you."

Gran, seeing the puzzled look on my face, adds: "My son, you would not understand since you do not have the gift. Besides, as I said before, the creator has given women from the beginning of time the special attributes that men in their self-conceit call wiles. Men would never understand. Is not the woman the mother of the man? It has always been so and it will always be. A ten-year-old girl can always hold her own against a male twice that age! Men think that they are wise. What they do not know or understand is that women are wiser! When a man sets out thinking that the woman is weaker, he makes himself even more vulnerable. He has let down his guard. While the woman continues to advance, he continues in the self-delusion that he is on top. This is not so. He is truly the lesser partner in any relationship and as a woman gains strength and authority, the man is obliged to give way. For example, take the farce called courtship. The man may think that he is simply getting to know the woman but the reverse is the truth. All along the woman will be indulging in what is known these days as marketing!

"If she has decided to choose the man who is wooing her, she will of course try to present her best face to the man. She allows the man to see what she knows he wants to see; but deep inside her is what is really important. In her basket of wiles are many faces: she puts them on and changes them at will, one face for the one she likes and another for the one she dislikes, yet another one for the one she loves and would ensnare and enslave for life. The poor man is soon blinded by love!

"I will tell you both a story," Gran said to Wehinmi and me without so much as pausing for breath. "There was the case of a courtship that had lasted two whole years. The poor man thought he knew his girl. He thought that she was not the deceptive type who would have three boyfriends at the same time. He saw her as a good, sweet and honest girl who would not hurt a fly. One evening when he was supposed to be at evening class and it was cancelled he decided to delight his sweetheart by paying her an unscheduled visit. He was shocked to find her in the arms of another boyfriend. Soon after that he discovered she was having frequent dates with yet another boy. Not surprisingly, he decided to avoid this girl in future. When this girl was let down by the third boyfriend, she made an attempt to make up with her first boyfriend – but he had learnt his lesson and would have none of it. I must add that there are just a few examples where it has been ordained that a particular boy and girl have been created for each other. Wisdom alone cannot help a man; he needs in addition the grace that comes from above.

"My dear children, I am so happy to see you both. Labi, it is a great joy to see you in real life. Wehinmi you look even more beautiful, radiant and happy. May God bless you both. I have been assured that I shall carry your children in my arms before I am called home. Do come and see me as often as you can. I shall always pray for you. Labi, have a safe journey to Lagos and please do not delay the wedding."

Back at Wehinmi's residence, she invites me into the sitting room. "Now my questions, Labi," she begins. "What exactly was your relationship with Phyllis? Did you fall in love with her? And she with you? Please be entirely frank with me. Did you kiss and cuddle regularly? Did you make love to her?"

I explain that most of this story has already been told but I did add that Phyllis liked me, but simply in a brotherly sense. "Had I given her encouragement the situation could have been different," I told her, "but there was always Frank. Besides, your face, Wehinmi, was always before me."

I admit that I did waiver once, but I was saved. One evening when I was really depressed and thinking about you, I felt sad, lonely and dejected. I thought that Uncle Bayo must have found you and I was just wasting my time. Who should come in just then? It was Phyllis. The moment she came in I knew that all was not well. She flopped into the chair, so unlike her usual self. She looked tired and dispirited. Without speaking, I could almost read her thoughts. She seemed to be saying, my man is not here, your sweetheart is not here, but we are here; we are fond of each other. We are all but in love. Why can't we at least make the best of it and enjoy ourselves instead of making ourselves miserable?

She then said aloud, 'I am a member of this household yet I have never been allowed to spend a night here. No one will put me off tonight. Whether you like it or not, I am going to sleep here tonight. I shall not have a lonely night today'.

I smiled at her affectionately, and went to the kitchen to make a pot of tea. Then I came back and poured two cups, offering her one. Although she accepted it, she looked at me pleadingly. 'Drink your tea first. We shall speak afterwards .' I said. After we had a few sips she stretched her hands across the table. I touched them, so lightly at first. Before I knew it I held them more firmly; then I started to caress them gently and lovingly. The lovely hand with its long fingers was soft and warm. I was all on fire. I wanted to get up and hold her to my chest, to kiss her and show her how much I understood her need and suffering as well as mine. She looked at me pleadingly, she seemed to be telling me her feelings reciprocated my own. However, I restrained myself. If I had risen from my seat we might have done something that we would regret for the rest of our lives. Why I started massaging her hand I simply don't know; perhaps more strangely, I started to hum so softly a West Indian calypso –her favourite - which calmed her so that she started to doze.

I then put her head on my lap while still caressing her. As she continued to sleep, she started to breathe softly and I gently placed her head on a cushion. I then went into the kitchen to cook her favourite dish of *egusi* soup and spinach with *eba*. When the table was set I gently woke her up. 'Phyllis, my dear sister come and eat,' I said. I watched her. 'I have enjoyed it, dear brother. You have saved me and my honour once again. May God bless you. Please telephone for a cab to take me home. Please bear with me. It won't happen again'. 'No, I have felt as you do from time to time; but we have resisted the urge and temptation for so long, why should we give in when we are nearing the finishing tape?' I told her.

"Her boyfriend Frank telephoned the next day. The truth was, he saved us from ourselves. In the frame of mind in which we both found ourselves something might have happened just before my return to Nigeria. That, my darling, is the honest truth regarding Phyllis and myself. It's the whole truth."

Wehinmi insists on returning to Lagos with me. However, I convince her not to. I promise to visit her again soon. She pleads and pleads, saying that after such a long separation we should always now be together. The night preceding my return to Lagos is a most painful one. Wehinmi insists that I should spend the night in her flat instead of going to the Catering Rest House. Somehow we overcome the temptation. We are together until the early hours of the morning. We limit ourselves to kissing and holding each other; it is deliciously painful, bitter and sweet at the same time. It seems inevitable that both of us should travel to and from Lagos and Warri frequently.

On Wehinmi's next visit to Lagos, we visit a lawyer friend. After hearing explanations about the circumstance of the wedding between Bayo and Wehinmi as well as the separation for over four years, the lawyer assures us that she can easily get a divorce. Kunle, the lawyer, telephones Bayo a few days later for an appointment. He goes to the meeting with a draft divorce settlement. When Bayo reads it and hears that Wehinmi and I are planning to become man and wife, he readily agrees. In addition, he promises to make a very generous wedding present to us in compensation for what he made Wehinmi go through. In due course the divorce comes through and Wehinmi is free to marry me.

The following weekend Wehinmi and I visit Ibadan to see her parents. Wehinmi's mother greets me warmly while recalling the romance between the two kids. She confesses that at the time she thought that it was just a childish infatuation. On hearing about Uncle Bayo's unfortunate predicament, Wehinmi's parents express sympathy for him. They both give their blessings to the proposed union between us. It is at this point that her father confesses that the letters I had sent to Wehinmi were destroyed by him. He then did not think that it was right that two young kids should engage in such correspondence. Wehinmi and I, as well as her mother, express disappointment at this, but in the happy mood of the occasion we do not want to dwell on past mistakes.

And thus, our relationship begins in earnest, a whirlwind kind of courtship followed very soon by the engagement and wedding, after the years of waiting. Ade, Bayo's cousin, is the best man. His wife, Yeside, also comes to the ceremony. For the best part of the time Wehinmi and I hold hands, with our eyes aglow.

We then travel to Jos for the honeymoon.

This time it is a real honeymoon. When Wehinmi relates the experiences of her last honeymoon, I feel moved. Both of us feel sorry for Uncle Bayo. Wehinmi said that he was always a real gentleman. Beyond the occasional kisses and embraces, she was never pressured; they even had separate bedrooms.

Wehinmi feels extremely sorry for him. Uncle Bayo was always sad not so much for his own condition but for his mother whose wish for a grandchild he could not gratify. Wehinmi adds that Bayo was always apologetic for the embarrassing situation he had put Wehinmi and Ade through. Wehinmi and I agree that we have no bitterness towards Uncle Bayo. We both assure him of a warm welcome to our home. Bayo's delight at the end of it all is very gratifying.

Gradually Wehinmi quickly settles down in Lagos and she refers to me as her husband and lover. She moves her business base to Lagos and the business keeps growing. Wehinmi's store has become the most popular place for George materials and Hayes head-ties.

Marriage suits both of us extremely well. One evening after our game of scrabble I recall 'the terrible girls' that were our classmates at St Peters School. I ask

Wehinmi about them one by one. 'Whatever happened to Mope, the besotted lover?" I ask. "Mope and Jide, her boyfriend, got married." "Jide is now an auto-mechanic and is doing extremely well. As in the past Mope continues to dote on him; only that now he has to compete for her attention with five kids. She has a shop on New Court Road, Ibadan."

"How about the dumb, pretty Joko?" I ask. "She is still pretty but no longer dumb: she caught a very eligible lawyer who is now a judge. She too is the mother of three kids, all boys; and I understand she basks in the admiration of four males," Wehinmi adds with a laugh.

"And the domineering Celina?" I enquire. "She is very much about and has not changed a bit. The last thing I heard about her was that she had just divorced her second husband. Since then she became attached to a much younger man who had lived abroad for many years. I suppose that he needs the guidance of a strong willed flirt like Celina to find his feet. With her young partner Celina may yet become a mother."

"Felicia the 'bush girl'," Wehinmi continues, "has returned home as I already told you. We are the best of friends now and you will get to see her again. We would never have imagined that she of all people would become so close a friend to me. It only goes to show that things and situations should not be taken at face value."

"And the 'terrible Ys'?," I ask. "Yewande and Yetunde continue to be terrible and dangerous. Their beauty continues to attract or rather entrap men, young and old; but marriage and happiness continue to elude them. They have both become widely known as home-breakers. No man or woman is safe from them. They continue to live fast lives, but age is fast catching up with them. Poor girls."

"Why do you call them poor?," I ask. "They are merely reaping what they sowed. Does not the morning show what the day will be like? They were never interested in marriage."

"No, the 'terrible Ys' prefer to hunt for rich men who will give them good time. Good time girls, that is what they were and still are and that is what they will always be. None of us could have ever foreseen what the future held. But going by what has happened the early beginnings pointed out what was likely to be.

"We, have cause to thank God," concludes Wehinmi. "By the way, are you looking forward to the visit to

Grandma tomorrow?" "Yes, very much so. My last visit with her was intriguing."

We wake to a very bright morning' and after breakfast set out for Grandma's place in Warri. We drive almost six hours with a short break at Ilesa. When we get there, Grandma is already on the veranda, her favourite relaxing corner. She asks for some more tea to be brought.

"How are you young folks settling down?" the old lady asks us. "Very well, Grandma. I am more in love with him than when I first met him," answers Wehinmi. I add, "Yes Grandma, Wehinmi is indeed a witch. She must have put a love potion in my food. I love her more and more. I cannot bear to let her out of my sight."

"I can very well believe that," Granny says with a giggle, "what with this protruding tummy. When is the young one expected? If only I could travel to Lagos and be around when the baby arrives. Unfortunately I am unable to travel any more. Make sure you send me news the very moment it happens."

After one week in Warri we return to Lagos; we travel in easy stages. We stop for two nights each in Benin City, Akure and Ibadan. After the trip, Wehinmi puts a temporary halt to her travels. She spends more time in bed. I spend a lot of evening time with her. It is nearing six in the evening one Saturday when Wehinmi asks to be taken to the hospital. It is a short labour. The child, a boy, arrives within two hours. I stay on in the hospital until both child and mother are asleep.

Two years later, we have a daughter. Three years after that the twins arrive, a boy and a girl. We then decide that we have a full house and our energy is concentrated on bringing up the children.

Wehinmi is always recalling the past, especially that Monday morning when she and I first met; and the heartache when she thought that I was lost to her. Again fate played a trick on us. When Wehinmi thought that at last she had found me it was not yet so. She had to wait another six years. But both Wehinmi and I have long come to the conclusion that the wait has been worth it. We are a contented and happy couple. It could not be otherwise. Wehinmi has in addition to me four lovely kids, a thriving and successful business, and I am doing extremely well in my own business. We decide to run the two businesses as one in our joint names.

When we reminisce we always conclude by saying that truly God has been gracious to us. Wehinmi adds that it has all come about as a result of genuine love and faithfulness. "Above all, we both have the fear of God in us. In return we have His grace which is all that any marriage can ask for."

VINDICATION

How it started

The bus was pulling up at the terminus as Gbade walked into the square. A smart young lady alighted. She walked ahead of Gbade, daintily picking her steps. She was clearly vivacious and full of life. Gbade had seen her face as she got down from the bus. Firmly imprinted on that face was the consciousness of her beauty and attractiveness.

Her school uniform showed that she was from the Princess College. Gbade quickened his pace and caught up with her. "Good evening, friend", he greeted her. "I bet we are going the same way." Before the young lady could answer he added, "I am Gbade. My tell-tale blazer has shown you that I am from Gregory High."

She answered in a soft and melodious voice that her name was Pero, "I hope that we retain the shield," she added.

"I'm afraid, that's not likely: our boys have prepared most seriously. The shield is ours," Gbade said. "We shall see", Pero answered quietly.

Gbade looked at her again. Her pointed nose and chiselled chin enhanced her beauty. She wore a very confident smile on her face. It was Gbade who spoke again. "I see you wear your beret on the left side, very much unlike your schoolmates."

"I am left handed," Pero answered.

"It's good to see something different," Gbade responded. He could not stop looking at the beauty by his side.

If she was aware of it she gave no indication. "Would you mind if I escort you home after the debate?" asked Gbade.

"Why would you take such trouble since you obviously live on the Island?" Pero replied.

"I will gladly walk you to the moon, if need be," Gbade quickly countered. "We shall see," Pero answered.

Princess College has been famous for years because of its beautiful lawns and gardens as well as for other good reasons. As they went through the gate, a pleasing fragrance from the roses and other flowers surrounding the lawns pervaded the compound. They walked into the large hall facing the main lawn. It was already half filled.

"Let's move to the front so that we can hear well," Pero said. The event of the evening was the final of the debate competition for Secondary Schools. The trophy had been won for two consecutive years by Princess College. They had high hopes of winning it for the third time running so that they could retain the trophy permanently.

The stage was already set. In the centre was the high table at which the panel of judges would sit. On the two sides were two smaller tables with chairs. Each set had at its front a rostrum. Soon the judges came in with the headmistress of Princess College carrying the coveted shield. As the chairperson, she immediately asked the two contesting pairs to come up to the podium. To Pero's surprise Gbade was one of the main speakers. The speakers were introduced and the rules for the debate were announced. Everyone applauded.Princess College as the defending champion would speak in favour of the motion, while Greg High as the opposing side would speak against.

The two young ladies in their well-groomed uniforms looked stunning; the two boys were wearing well starched trousers and smart brown blazers. The chief proposer of the motion was given a maximum of fifteen minutes to speak, as was the chief opposer in response. Thereafter, the two seconders were given ten minutes each to make rebuttals and additional points.

These were followed by contributions from the floor. The headmistress then summarised the main points made by both sides as well as those from the audience.

At the end of the speeches, loud applause filled the hall. Within the next five minutes, members of the panel of judges appeared to have agreed on the scores; then the audience was asked to vote, if only to confirm the verdict. As with the trend of the speeches, more hands, including those of some of the girls, went up in support of the opposing team. And so, Princess College was not able to retain the shield permanently.

Gbade's partner was a senior boy, a sixth former, and it was he who went forward to collect the shield and shake hands with all the judges. He then shook hands with the two young ladies. He raised the trophy to yet another round of applause.

The headmistress of Princess College rounded up the proceedings by congratulating the winning team, thanking both teams and everybody present. She also advised all the schools and colleges present to start preparations for next year's competition as early as possible. Gbade and his partner came down from the stage hand in hand, the latter still clutching the shield.

Gbade walked down briskly towards the waiting young lady. Although her college had lost, Pero's congratulations and handshake were warm and spontaneous. The look on both faces spoke very clearly: the pair had fallen in love at first sight. Both of them walked silently to the bus stop. The tender glances and smiles were as eloquent as spoken words.

As Pero got into the bus, Gbade followed her. Immediately they sat down they held hands. Gbade felt Pero's soft fingers in his palm. He felt very happy. From the mainland terminus he walked her right to the door of her house. The adventure had started. So it continued afterwards. Before long, everyone began to notice the inseparable pair.

Within two years their love blossomed and by the time Gbade left High School they had pledged undying love to each other. Thus started a courtship that lasted eight long years. It was inevitable that there would be lovers' quarrels. Gbade was a dashing and handsome young-man who was highly gifted. Pero too, with her ever smiling pretty face, always cool and unruffled, was bound to attract the admiration of other young men.

However, their friendship survived with only a

partial break of very brief duration. It was a most romantic relationship. They would spend hours together dreaming of a bright and happy future. The support from members of their two families gave the couple a great deal of encouragement. On some weekends during term Gbade and Pero would go for picnics, excursions or dramatic and cultural events with other students from the two colleges and other secondary schools.The pattern and variety of events during the long vacations were different. The two lovers were always together under one pretext or another. They obviously enjoyed each other's company.

During one of the picnics an incident occurred. As the pair walked along a narrow footpath they saw ahead of them three young ladies. One of them was sitting on the ground with her back against a tree. The other two were applying some dressings to her ankle. The injured young lady appeared to be in pain. When Gbade and Pero got to the spot, one of the two girls asked Gbade for help. Gbade deftly removed the bandage and examined the swollen ankle. He said that the crepe bandage had been applied too tightly. In an instant he opened his first aid kit, applied some embrocation and bandaged the injured ankle again.

Next he produced his flask of cold water. He applied a little water to the young lady's brow after which he offered her a cup of cold water.

While he was attending to the injured girl, the parties on both sides introduced themselves. They walked down the path led by the two friends. At the rear was the injured girl hopping on one foot with her arms around the shoulders of Gbade and Pero. Just as the two parties were about to take their leave, the injured one, whose name was Nide, said excitedly, "I now remember, you are the troop leader of the second Island Troop which won the First Aid competition last quarter. I thought I had seen the face before. I took part in the competition. I belong to the Third Guide Company." The three young ladies said thank you and Gbade and Pero left.

Nide walked home in a daze, stopping from time to time. She did not see her aunt who was sitting quietly in the living room. She had almost walked by when the aunt called out. "Nide, whatever is the matter? You look strange. I hope all is well."

"All is well Auntie, except for my injured ankle. We had a wonderful time at the picnic." she answered. "Come and have your meal," invited Auntie Sade. "

The table is already set."

Nide was unusually quiet during the meal. She left the table hurriedly pleading tiredness. She flopped onto the bed in her room. Then started talking to herself: "What is happening to me. I feel so excited and happy; but at the same time I feel sad and down". Gbade's picture filled her thoughts. She continued her thinking: "His presence puts new life into me. I would love to be with him every moment of my life. That pretty girl beside him, would she allow it? Because of her, would he have eyes for any other female? I am also pretty. I can hold my own. I'll try. We shall see. The mere thought of him makes me tingle all over. What is this madness that has come over me? Have I fallen in love with him? I am no longer in control of myself. May heaven help me." Try as she might, she could not sleep, thinking of him and the strange effect he had on her.

About a week after the incident, the injured young lady (now without the crepe bandage) visited Gbade's house. She had come to thank him. She repeated the thank you call on two other occasions, much to the amusement and consternation of Gbade. When Gbade mentioned the visit to Pero she smiled mischievously. She joked, "We must be hopeful that no more sprains will occur in the future."

"What is that supposed to mean"? queried Gbade, to which Pero replied, "If a handsome young man will caress my foot while bandaging my ankle, I will oblige and sprain the ankle every other day. I shall of course insist on a good looking first-aider."

"Someone is jealous," observed Gbade.

"Do you blame me? I would not want any pretty and smart young woman dancing round my boyfriend."

"Come off it. What time would I have left when I have to report every morning at Greg High and in the evening I have to present myself dutifully and promptly at seven o'clock at Pero's house," replied Gbade.

"You just watch it. If I ever catch Miss Pretty calling on you again, all hell will be let loose," Pero countered.

"You have nothing to fear, Miss. You already have me on the leash."

Nide Makes Her Move
Nide set out to find out all about Gbade. What she learnt made her to want him more than ever. She was upset when it was also confirmed by many that the pretty Pero of Princess High had been his sweetheart for some time. Everyone spoke of the suitability of

the two being lovers. "What a lovely pair," they all said. The more she heard, the more disconsolate she became.

"I know what to do," she said to herself. She had found out that every Tuesday without fail Pero attended netball practice at the High between five and six in the evening. "Next Tuesday at five, the coast will be clear," she thought. "That will be the time to pay Gbade a visit."

So she was there on the following Tuesday on the dot of five. Gbade was in his room doing his homework when he was informed by his younger brother, teasingly, that a 'charming lady' was waiting for him in the living room. 'Who could that be?' he wondered. As he entered, there she was, sitting calmly. She stood up and flashed a bewitching smile at him. Before Gbade could speak she went on, "I have been extremely busy and so I could not repeat my visit before now. By the way, my name is Omonide. My friends call me Nide. I hope you too will call me that."

"It's an unusual name," Gbade answered, "but it sounds pretty . My name is Gbade. Shall we go out into the garden so that we can sit on the bench under the tree?"

Nide agreed to this. After they were comfortably seated she said, "I have come to see you. I need advice."

"What is it? I will be delighted to help if I can," replied Gbade.

"How do I start?" "Yes, I am listening."

"From the day I set my eyes on you, life for me has not been the same," Nide confided. "I am both happy and unhappy. I wish I could be with you every minute of my life. Sometimes I find it difficult to breathe for thinking of you."

Gbade raised his hand as if wanting to speak. "Please hear me out. Do not interrupt me," Nide pleaded. "I know it is not modest for a lady to speak to a gentleman in this manner, but I must. I have had many agonising hours. The truth is that I had never in all my life felt like I do and have done since setting eyes on you. I was smitten the moment I set eyes on you. Although I had suspected it, I became sure in my mind that I was in love with you. I am madly in love. But something tells me that I have come too late. Something tells me that if you had not earlier met a girl named Pero, things might have been different. What do I do now? Please advise me."

Gbade looked at her quizzically but tenderly. He was in a quandary. His look was full of pity and dismay. For many minutes he did not speak. When he did, it was in a tremulous voice. "Dear young lady I am sorry, terribly sorry that you should feel that way about me. I have already given my love to Pero. She has all of me. We have promised undying love for each other."

Nide looked pale and faint. "I understand," she said. "Please do not harbour any ill feeling towards me. I am not a bad girl. I had never fallen in love before. But I had always known that, when I do, it would overwhelm me. It has. I love you and I always will. Please remember me sometimes and pray for me. Perhaps you would like to have me as a sister. In that capacity I can be in your company and hers at times. That will make me happy, very happy. Think about it.

One day I shall be interested to hear what you think of that proposal."

Before Gbade could think of a suitable answer, she had got up and walked away. For many minutes Gbade sat all alone beneath the tree. He knew that what the girl said was true. He could feel it. He knew that she was in earnest. He was overcome with pity. Two in love with the same man. What a hopeless and helpless tangle. What will become of the poor girl? He had a premonition that something would happen. If only one could see the future? The poor girl. May heaven send her someone else to love. What will Pero say?" These were the thoughts that ran through his mind. He looked at his watch. He was already running late. Pero would expect him at the school gate to walk her home after netball.

He dashed off for Princess College. He arrived just in time. Pero and her friends were just coming out. "You are puffing dear. What happened? You should have left home earlier. Have you seen a ghost? Aren't you pleased to see me? You look dazed." He had no answer to the barrage of questions. What could he say? Pero looked at him with amused puzzlement. Both of them decided to let the matter rest.

When Pero finished at Princess College she decided to attend a Teacher Training College some hundred miles away from home. While Gbade was in support of her taking the course, he had some misgivings. Understandably, he thought that his sweetheart might be snatched from him by some enterprising young men far away from home. The possibility looked stronger as there was a university near the Teacher Training College. Besides, this was Pero's first trip away from home. The only redeeming feature was that Tara, Pero's classmate at Princess College, was also going to the same college. With Pero and Tara acting as chaperones to each other Gbade felt that he had a measure of security. That thought also gave him comfort.

The course was to last four years. All too soon the first two years flew by. During this period the two love birds travelled frequently between the two towns to see each other. Whenever they were together it was all bliss and happiness. The constant partings, however, brought pain and sadness.

Two years after Pero went to the Teacher's College Gbade won a government scholarship to study in England for four years. Both of them were in a dilemma. Students of the Teacher Training College were not allowed to get married during their period of training. Pregnancy while at college had always resulted in expulsion. To make matters worse, there were frequent stories of smart English girls ensnaring young African men.

Two weeks before Gbade's departure for England, Pero sent an urgent message to him to come over to the college. On arrival she clung to him with an anguished face. She came straight to the point. "Unless we get married secretly, before your departure, this may be goodbye forever."

"Why should that be"? Gbade asked.

"What with all the stories about girls in England, I cannot afford to lose you," Pero answered. After consulting the parents on both sides, a registry marriage took place ten days before Gbade's departure. Fortunately the customary enquiries on both sides had previously been made. Needless to say, given the circumstances, the marriage was not consummated. The night before Gbade's departure was a most agonising one for the couple. They kissed, cuddled, hugged and clung to each other for hours.

And so Gbade flew off to England. Thus began two years of further separation. This time, four thousand rather than one hundred miles separated them. The two years felt like ten. Letters of endearment and protestations of enduring loyalty flew backwards and forwards. It was a very sad and trying period for both of them.

Life dragged on until that July morning when Pero flew into London to join her husband. The joyful reunion defied description. As Pero emerged from the immigration department at the airport, she and Gbade rushed into each other's arms, hugging and kissing. For minutes they clung together without speaking. Then Pero started to cry. Gbade was startled "Why all this crying, now that we are together at last?" He calmed her down and steered her towards the waiting taxi. Gbade had eighteen months to complete his course when Pero arrived in London.

The couple both hoped to return home with a baby, or at least with Pero pregnant. But try as they might there was no sign of pregnancy. They, as well as relations on both sides back home, were disappointed. The couple had to wait ten years before their first child, a girl, arrived. They later had two other children, one boy and another girl. Gbade and Pero were quite well and happy, especially as both of them were progressing well in their careers. Gbade was already a director in his company while Pero had become the headmistress of her school. All their children were brilliant and got on splendidly in their studies.

Everything was going smoothly until one fateful evening when Gbade went to his club. Some members were commiserating with one of their colleagues who had just got married. It was discovered that the new bride was not a virgin. The naïve Gbade was unable to join in the conversation due to his ignorance of the subject. When all the others, except the affected member who was still brooding over his mug of beer, had left, Gbade moved closer to him.

Gbade asked why he was so sure that his wife was not a virgin. With a look of disgust he answered that there had been no obstruction, no screaming and no pain. She just clung to him and appeared to be enjoying herself. "When I, as the affronted husband, asked what it all meant, her attitude and answer were even more devastating." "She asked me, 'Do you expect a lady of my age not to have had sexual experience? Wake up my man; these are modern times'."

The whole episode set Gbade thinking. Although his own wife at their first encounter had not spoken like that, but as far as he could recall there was no impediment whatsoever; neither was there any blood nor screams, nor did his wife complain about any pain. He really loved his wife and did not want the peace within their home disturbed. For this reason he made no reference to this episode.

However, Gbade became resentful. Distrust of his wife started to creep in. He was often moody and kept aloof most of the time. He stayed out more than he normally did and when at home he busied himself with his books. Husband and wife started to drift apart. It was Pero who called attention to this new development. She came and nestled by him on the settee. "Darling, I feel neglected. It's not like you to stay out late day after day. You used to be the home type and I know that you really enjoyed the time we spent together. Now whenever you are home you bury yourself in the study. What have I done to upset you? Please hold me in your arms and kiss me. Your neglect of me is killing me slowly," Pero remonstrated.

Gbade was normally a forthright person and he could not lie. He narrated the episode at the club and referred to their first sexual encounter. He ended on the note that he was most unhappy. He reminded her that during their courtship she was always restraining him so that they could have a most enjoyable and befitting consummation after marriage. He again confessed his ignorance of such matters as he had had no sexual experience before that first encounter in London. What he gathered after making enquiries from his friends in the medical profession made him doubtful as to his wife's truthfulness and chastity. "I was told that a bloodless consummation was just not possible," he ended with a doleful face.

"Supposing there had been an accident," countered Pero.

"What sort of accident?" asked Gbade, adding, "Please do not trivialize this issue or treat me like a fool." Pero claimed to have read about such an accident in a book some time ago.

"Please Pero let us end this conversation. I do not want the peace in this home shattered. Our children and junior relations look up to us. Even if we are not happy as a couple let us pretend to be. When we got married we did so for better or for worse. I am prepared to accept my lot. I shall leave you to your conscience."

The discontent lingered for quite a while. It was a most trying period for both of them. During that period all they could do was to pray.

Late one night Gbade and Pero were watching a film on the television. In it a tyrant who was chieftain of a village had detained some young women who were protesting against the ill-treatment of their menfolk who were opposed to him. The most beautiful of the women was the fiancée of the leader of the dissidents. While all the other girls were herded into a hut, the tyrant ordered that this girl be brought to his quarters. He raped and defiled her before sending her home. At this point, for an inexplicable reason, Gbade looked at Pero. Their eyes met. Although no words were uttered, the look in Gbade's eyes were as good as spoken words. He seemed to be asking, "Was that what happened?" Then, utter silence.

After the film ended Pero got up and tenderly embraced Gbade. While still clinging to him she said very quietly and in a subdued tone: "Darling I have always been faithful to you." Gbade was bewildered. All he could say at that point was, "My good wife, I believe you."

When Gbade eventually went to bed, he could not sleep. All sorts of thoughts went through his mind. Could Pero have been raped? Or in a moment of temptation, during the long separation, could she have succumbed to someone else due to loneliness? Although the great love for his wife eventually prevailed, the doubts and mistrust of the past resurfaced. It lingered for some time. The resultant effect was renewed heartache for both Gbade and Pero.

Some nights after the television film, Gbade was woken up by Pero. She told him that he had been shouting aloud in his sleep. "Stop violating her; stop this defilement. She is my wife". These were the words Pero said Gbade had shouted. "What was happening"? Pero asked.

"I was dreaming. It was such a bad dream. May God preserve us and sustain the peace in this home." Although pressed by Pero, Gbade did not say anything further.

The unease and tension returned. The following night Gbade had another dream. A total stranger suddenly appeared. He prostrated before him and asked for 'forgiveness for a great wrong he did me and mine.' I could not see the face of the stranger clearly. 'What's wrong? I do not know you nor do I understand what you are talking about.' He then woke up with a start.

When Gbade related this dream to Pero he noticed that she too was startled. In addition there was a look of fear on her face. Gbade's understanding of feminine body language had always been uncanny. The startled look mingled with fear on Pero's face provoked in him a lot of thoughts. On the spur of the moment he asked if Pero could spare some minutes to listen to one of the legends in his family. "Sure," replied Pero, "You know I am interested and would love to know everything about you and your family."

"Sit down then and make yourself comfortable" said Gbade. "When we were kids we used to visit the village often to spend our holidays during the long vacations and my grandfather usually told us stories. I want you to listen to one of them which I found very fascinating."

Gbade then recounted the legend of the Queen's basket[2]: "Labo was the first daughter of Oba Afun and was therefore known as Bere. One morning the Oba did not emerge as usual from his chamber. The courtiers did not know what to do. They asked Bere to enter the royal chamber to find out what was wrong. The king said a horrendous thing had happened. All his powers came from just touching a special basket

[2] This legend is one of those included in "The Quest for the Rare Leaf and other Yoruba tales" published in parallel with this edition.

134

that had been entrusted to him by the late Queen. 'Without the Queen's basket I am nothing,' he said. 'Every morning when I wake up the first thing I do is to touch the basket.' Because he had weighty issues that day he thought he would obtain extra power and discernment by touching the contents. He opened the basket and found the contents spoiled. Bere pointed out that physical state of the contents could not diminish his powers because they depended on the strength of his faith. She asked him what the packets dropped into the basket contained.

" 'They were the trophies of virtue of our womenfolk. Whenever they got married their *ibale* (the sign that their virginity was intact) were sent home as proof of their virtue and the high standard of their upbringing. This was the white cloth stained by blood during consummation of the marriage. Such brides were respected by their families on both sides and they were given presents. For brides who failed there were awful consequences.

"Asked why the cloths had rotted, the king explained that they used special dyes and that the art of making them had got lost. As Bere knew all about herbs she promised her father that she would find the right ones to solve the problem. The king appointed Bere custodian of the Queen's basket and the king emerged to be greeted by his cheering courtiers."

"What an interesting story," said Pero. Before Gbade could reply she went on, "Why have you never told me the story before?"

"I don't know," answered Gbade. After a little pause he added, as if an afterthought, "Maybe it had never occurred to me to tell you. I'm happy that you like it." There was another pause before Gbade added: "As you well know the music that issues forth from an *agidigbo* musical instrument, though melodious and enthralling, is not unlike the proverbs of the elders. Only the wise can interpret them and it takes a very discerning heart to keep in step with its melody."

"You sound very deep in philosophical tonight. Let us go to bed oh Solomon." For the best part of the night Pero was unable to sleep. All sorts of thoughts went through her mind. She tossed and turned in bed. Try as she might, sleep would not come until the early hours of the morning.

* * *

Bayo and the curse

Meanwhile a man by the name of Bayo had returned to the town of Agbodu after over three decades away in the big cities. His arrival had been causing a stir and, but for the two recent tragedies that befell him, the occasion would have been one for great celebration. Those who had knew him remembered him as the brightest student in Agbodu High School, intellectually gifted, handsome and talkative. Many young ladies as well as their mothers were disappointed when he left for the Teacher Training College about thirty years ago.

Now that he had returned to be the principal of Agbodu High School, the first African to be so appointed, many thought that wonders would start to happen. The stories making the rounds, however, were that the Bayo who had returned was quite a different person. Not only was he extremely sad; he was aloof. Only a distant relation and her pretty young daughter, Tomi, were welcomed as visitors in the principal's house. After school hours he kept mostly indoors. It was said that he was very unhappy.

Apart from the two ladies mentioned, there was a young male student who helped with the house cleaning. All the other chores were left to the two women. It was, therefore, very likely that pretty Tomi should fall in love with Bayo. She and her mother were able to arouse him from his state of lethargy. He started to show affection for Tomi. It was clear that he was fond of her. But that was as far as it went.

It was reported that Bayo had said that for Tomi's sake there would be no talk of union between them. He would not wish the poor girl to be the next victim of the tragedy that inevitably befell any lady who fell in love with him, or was in any way involved with him. Six months before Bayo decided to return home, his only child, a nineteen-year old daughter had been raped and taken her own life. The mother, Bayo's late wife whom he had married secretly had doted on the daughter, pined away and also eventually died. Before Bayo got married to this unfortunate lady he had had a previous attachment. Some three months before the proposed marriage, when Bayo decided to ask for her hand, tragedy struck. The woman had been raped by a notorious philanderer and she had to leave the town because of the stigma. It would seem that any woman who fell in love with Bayo was bound for misfortune or disaster. It was generally believed that a curse had been put on him.

As a result of the pressure exerted on Bayo by Tomi and her mother it was decided that a diviner should be approached to determine the source of Bayo's curse, if it was true that he had one. The diviner's finding made matters worse: it was that in times past Bayo had offended a man, highly favoured by the *irunmales*. It was said that the man was a descendant of one of the important *irunmales*. Unless and until that person lifted the curse on Bayo, any woman who fell in love with him, especially if he reciprocated the love, would meet also meet disaster. Two other diviners were consulted and they confirmed the findings of the first one.

Tomi and the mother did not relent in their efforts. Eventually they prevailed on Bayo to pursue the course of action advised. It was only then that he confessed that he had raped a young woman a long time back , one of his juniors at the Teacher Training College. The young lady already had a fiancé – he believed – when the sad event occurred. The man and the raped woman later got married. The man in question had become very famous and important. Bayo was ashamed and reluctant to approach Pero, for it was she, and he therefore made no attempt to find the couple.

Now due to the pressure and his eagerness to

get married and raise a family Bayo decided to go in search of Pero's friend, Tara. There was, however, another hurdle he had to overcome. When the sad event occurred, Pero had not taken Tara into her confidence due to the shame and stigma of rape. He rightly assumed that Tara's horror when she learned what happened might now alienate her from him.

According to Tomi's mother, Bayo had no alternative than to swallow his pride and tell Tara what he had done and seek her forgiveness; this should open the door for the much-needed assistance. It was Tomi's mother who eventually convinced Bayo to follow her on the visit to Tara. After several visits and much persuasion Tara agreed to broach the matter with Pero.

One Saturday afternoon, just before lunch, the gateman announced the arrival of a visitor for Pero. When Pero enquired who it was, it turned out to be Tara. Gbade and Pero had not seen or heard from Tara for a number of years. They were, therefore, surprised but pleased to see her. The three of them enjoyed a hearty lunch and talked about old times.

Good manners dictated that Gbade should excuse the two friends as they might have confidences to exchange after such a long separation. Besides, Gbade had observed that Tara was not at ease. He guessed that she wanted to be alone with Pero. As soon as Gbade left them, Tara disclosed that her mission was rather delicate and that she suspected that she might be seen as the bringer of bad news. She told her that Bayo, whom she had not seen in years, had come to see her begging to be brought to see Gbade and Pero regarding a very sensitive and pressing matter. Tara further disclosed that when she pressed Bayo, he had confessed the rape. He was in a bad way and desperately needed help.

The aggrieved Pero understandably refused point blank to discuss about Bayo, let alone receive him. She stressed that there was no way she would agree to see him. She was peeved that Bayo had told Tara - and perhaps others - about her predicament.

"Why?" asked Tara, "after all we were his friends."

Pero retorted: "While you and he may be from the same town and are related, I am definitely not his friend. A good man would not have callously raped a lady he regarded as a friend. We were mere college mates. Besides, there is another big hurdle…..I never had the courage to take Gbade into confidence in this difficult matter. Often I thought that Gbade suspected something but I always insisted on my faithfulness to him – which is true. How could I now face him and make such a confession? To help the scoundrel who was the cause of all my trouble. Over and over again Gbade has reaffirmed his love for me; but I always had the feeling that he did not trust me. I would, therefore, not risk wrecking our happiness."

Pero was adamant and refused to give her cooperation. Understandably, she was still hurt, offended and humiliated and she believed that Bayo should be allowed "to stew in his own juice." Pero later told Gbade that Tara left rather disappointed and crestfallen.

The following Saturday Tara repeated her visit, this time accompanied by two women, both of them unknown to Pero. Fortunately Gbade was not around. Gbade was told later that after much pleading and pressure from the two ladies Pero agreed that Bayo could come. Pero's fears that her secret had become public knowledge was confirmed. Despite the pressure from Tomi and her mother, Bayo continued to refuse to meet Pero. However, after much hesitation, he agreed to see Gbade. He wrote a letter to Gbade with a copy to Pero.

But Bayo tried to be too clever and he withheld the

original letter intended for Gbade. Pero's copy was duly sent. This was a subtle attempt to blackmail Pero should the need later arise.

On a fateful Saturday afternoon, when Bayo knew that Gbade would still be away at work, he called on Pero. Predictably he got a very cold welcome. He said he would wait for Gbade no matter how late he got home. Pero felt trapped. She advised that although Bayo could stay in the neighbourhood, she needed two hours to serve her husband's dinner and prepare him for the inevitable. Bayo had no option than to agree. Both of them were caught in the same trap. What eventually saved the day was the deep and abiding affection that had always existed between Gbade and

Pero. Before Gbade's arrival, Pero had primed the servants to be extremely careful and be at their best. This was to put Gbade in a good mood.

Pero offered to say the prayer preceding the meal. In addition to thanking the good Lord for the meal as well as the good health to enjoy it, she added her appreciation for the love and care shared by them both. During the meal and after, she talked about what she had done all day and asked Gbade about his day. They spent some time exchanging these pleasantries.

Very sensitive person that he was, Gbade quickly observed that Pero's mood, though good, was unusual. "Darling," he asked gently, "is anything the matter?"

She quickly replied: "Do you remember the other day when you reaffirmed that you would always love me. You went on to say on that occasion that love is patient and kind and you added that it always trusts and protects". At this stage, she got up from her chair, embraced Gbade lovingly and knelt at his feet holding his knees. "Darling," she continued, "I wish to ask you for perhaps the greatest favour I will ever ask. I hope you will grant it. Without your love I have always treasured, my life would be empty."

"What is this all about?" asked Gbade. "You know

that in spite of our differences every now and again, I will always love you. We are one now, how could I not love you with all my heart? You are part of me and I hope that I am part of you. Go ahead and ask, you already have whatever you want from me."

"You are too good to me. May the good Lord continue to bless you and our marriage," Pero continued. "You will recall your dream some time ago when you said that the man who came between us would come and ask for forgiveness. In the attempt to cover my shame, I said that no such person existed. But that was not true. Please forgive me. Hold me in your arms. Hold me tightly. The man is here. When he has explained himself you will see that I was blameless. He needs our joint forgiveness. Please for my sake hear what he has to say. May the good Lord guide you."

Gbade lifted her up gently and embraced her tenderly. "I had always been acutely aware there was a barrier between us. Bring the man so that the barrier may be removed for all time."

"Thank you, thank you, my love. I have never been unfaithful to you. Before I invite him in let the words come from my lips first. I was raped! No self-respecting wife would ever admit to such a thing. Pity me. Hear him out before you judge me."

"Who says I want to judge you? Gbade replied. "If I were to do that I would also be judging myself since we are now one body. Darling, stop upsetting yourself. I am convinced of your innocence and goodness. You should have taken me into confidence long before now. We would both have been saved the crises we went through. Please invite the visitor in." At this point Pero asked one of the servants to go next door and bring Bayo in.

Bayo came in, unsteady on his feet. In an attempt to prostrate himself he fell flat on his face. "Sir, I cannot look you or your good wife in the eyes to make this confession. I need your forgiveness so that I can regain my sanity and start to live a normal life again. Please let me tell it all before you interrupt. I am Bayo. I was three years ahead of Pero and Tara at the Teacher Training College. Although Tara is not a relation of mine, we both come from Agbodu. I have known her from childhood. When she introduced her friend, Pero, to me I fell for her instantly. I became her slave. I decided to woo and win her; but it was never to be. On the first occasion I made my feelings known Pero told me that she could not love me or any man other than her first true love to

146

whom she was already engaged. She told me never to address her on the subject again. She even threatened to withdraw the friendship she had given me because of her friendship with Tara. I gave her my solemn promise never to broach the subject again. Despite that promise, I remained her admirer. I was brooding and waiting. I was always kind and helpful to both Tara and Pero. In time Pero came to regard me as a trusted friend. I was, however, planning and watching.

"As I said previously, Tara and I come from the same town. This allowed me to act and behave as Tara's relation. Two months before my thirtieth birthday, I had asked Tara and Pero to make all the refreshments to be served and to play hostesses at my party. About a week or so before the party, Tara took ill and was confined to the college clinic. It took a lot of entreaties and cajoling to get her discharged two days before the birthday celebration. I manipulated it all because I knew that if Tara could not attend, Pero would not. As Tara was still weak as a result of her illness, a lot of the responsibility fell on Pero. Tara spent a lot of time resting and lying down. This threw Pero and me together a lot. Often Pero would tactfully extricate herself from my 'accidental' embraces. After a stern warning from her, I stopped

147

attempting to embrace her. My fear was that I would drive her away. Considering my secret plan I could not risk that.

"On the fateful day of my birthday party, although Tara got dressed and put on a bold face though, she was still not well. She was forced to sit down most of the time while Pero shouldered all the responsibilities as a good and trusted friend. As the party went on far into the night, it was arranged for Tara and Pero to spend the night in my guest room. As the best student in the final year I was already serving as assistant lecturer and had been given a house in the official quarters. As the evening wore on Tara's condition started to get worse. Fortunately some doctor friends were present. She was given some medication to tide her over until the next morning. A sedative was prescribed for her along with other medicines to ensure that she had a comfortable night.

"Pero and the house help were washing and tidying up and Pero was completely exhausted. I offered to make a chocolate drink to enable us sleep peacefully. Unknown to Pero I had put some of Tara's sedative into her cup. I then suggested that she should lie down for a while on the settee while the house help and I finished the cleaning up. We were to call her when we finished so that she could join Tara in the guest room. Unsuspecting, the poor victim agreed.

"After the house help had gone to the servants' quarters I sat on a chair pretending to be reading a book. I was in fact waiting for the sedative in Pero's drink to take effect. When her breathing had become regular I shook her to see if she was in a deep sleep. I then started to remove her clothes. Pero tried to get up but she could not. Besides, I was already pinning her down firmly. Soon after that, I started fondling and caressing her. At this point Pero let out a blood curdling scream. Alas, no one could hear her. The house help was safely in the servants' quarters many yards away and Tara had been heavily sedated. I had added a little bit to what the doctor had instructed so she was in no position to hear Pero's scream, let alone come to her assistance. After Pero's futile struggle I had my way and raped her. Poor Pero was wailing and weeping profusely. I fled the room."

Gbade now asked, "Pero, what did you do then?" Pero, with her head bowed, answered in a tremulous voice full of emotion. "Although I was sedated, I struggled to a sitting position. I was most uncomfortable. I was in great pain. I managed to get up on my feet and make for the guest room. But then it dawned on me that unless I cleaned the mess on the settee and floor, Tara and the house help would realise what took place. In my anxiety not to leave any trace I forgot my giddiness, agony and anger. I concentrated on cleaning the blood stain from both the settee and the carpet.

"Afterwards I dragged myself to the guest room, taking great care not to wake Tara up. I did not want her to see me in my pitiable condition. I went into the bathroom and struggled to clean myself up. I achieved it, between crying and cursing. I got into bed beside Tara. I was shaking all over. Needless to say I could not sleep. An indescribable anger possessed me. Much as I would have loved to have fallen into a deep sleep, to make me oblivious, if only temporarily, of my affliction, sleep fled from me. The harder I tried the more wide awake I became. I pinched myself to see if I was indeed awake or perhaps I was in a dream. It was a bad nightmare.

"How could this happen to me? My virginity which I had guarded zealously for over twenty four years had been taken away. Why did Satan choose to visit me in the guise of a man called Bayo? I had been eagerly looking forward to the night when my marriage with Gbade would be consummated. I had already been imagining the big hug of pleasure and approval which Gbade would lavish on me in deep appreciation of my virginity. I was going to flaunt my virginity and dazzle my lover, my husband anew. Now, that could never be. Instead, all that I would get from him was perhaps contempt and derision, if not worse. The shame would be so overwhelming it would kill me. The horror! The disaster! How my life had been changed dramatically. Why was I subjected to such indignity, insult and humiliation? Poor me, my 'ibale' would never be sent back to my parents. My name would be forever blotted out from the list of virtuous women within my husband's family and mine. What a disaster. Could I ever face Gbade again, I asked myself? It was the longest night of my life. I tossed and turned in bed. Help me God, I cried continuously but silently throughout that never to be forgotten, traumatic night.

"It suddenly occurred to me that the cleaning in the lounge might not have been properly done. It would not do to leave any tell-tale signs. I quickly got up and despite my emotional bruise I meticulously cleaned both the settee and the carpet all over again – to wipe away the traces of my shame, as it were. I thought that the exertion would wear me out and help me to sleep. But alas, when I got back into bed, sleep would still not come. And so my thoughts started drifting on and on. Love making, I had heard described, was a most enjoyable sport and a blissful experience between two lovers. Certainly what had happened to me two hours or so before was not love-making. The two parties involved were not even friends, let alone lovers. It was sport all right for one person, the demon, the animal who brutalized and violated me. I swore to myself that one day he would pay for it. Little did I know that I was making a prophesy. My sad experience was accompanied by physical and spiritual pain. An indelible mark was left on my heart. I had been ravished and violated. I felt thoroughly soiled. Unless heaven came to my rescue I would be damned forever. But above all, I asked myself how I might explain it to Gbade, especially with all my preaching over the years for the need to wait patiently for the special night at our honeymoon. I consoled myself by saying that an explanation would not be necessary. Heaven would come to my rescue. What had I done to deserve this ordeal and stigma? Did I sin in a former life? Even if it were so, is this punishment not too harsh? And so, the long night wore on. Yet, I could not sleep.

"In the morning, due to a sense of great shame and the humiliation I did not and could not say a word to Tara. We were driven to our hostel by my devilish tormentor. Throughout the short drive no conversation took place. The others might have attributed the silence to tiredness but I knew otherwise. Fortunately it was a Sunday. I pleaded tiredness and promptly went into my room.

"I got into the bath and scrubbed myself thoroughly, as if to wipe off the previous night's dastardly act. I was weeping, moaning, sighing and cursing my tormentor all the time. I started talking to myself in the bathroom. My life had been ruined. What do I tell my husband? Can I disclose this to anyone, let alone Gbade? Then a terrible thought assailed me. What if I become pregnant? Should I abandon my studies and run away? Should I commit suicide and end it all? I lived the next few weeks in a daze mixed with terror. Whenever I was alone I would back over the past. Since Gbade's departure for England I had become lonely and miserable.

"Thank God for Tara. With her constant companionship it was not easy for the wolves to get at me. The stupid rule against marriage made it impossible for me to disclose my true status. I was hemmed in.

"I should not forget that two days after the party Bayo came, ostensibly to thank us. He had tactfully kept away from us until then. About a month later he asked to have a few words with me. Tara withdrew from the room. He started by offering apologies for raping me. He said that what he did was caused by genuine love. He could not open the subject of love with me again as I told him that I was already engaged. Besides, I had earlier forbidden him not to talk to me about love or anything else again. He thought that by raping me I would be forced into marrying him as I would not like anybody else to know. As this tirade went on I stared at him with unseeing eyes. I told him that but for the shame and stigma, I would have reported him to the police. I went on to say that if I became pregnant, I would not hesitate to abort the pregnancy. I made it clear to him that I could not marry a man like him under any circumstance. I ended on the note that I might never marry as I would not like to deceive my fiancé or disclose this humiliating and disgraceful occurrence to him or anyone else. I was not even able to tell him I was already married as I thought that it was not beyond his despicable character to tell the college authorities if only to further damage my life. I ended saying that on no account was he to speak to me again. In reply, he said haltingly that there was no risk of pregnancy as he had been well protected. I sent him off with many curses.

"As soon as Tara got well she observed that all was not well with me. When she asked if I was ill I assured her that I was fine. Yet I could not get over the nightmare. I had never been so sad or so wretched in all my life. Traces of this might have shown in my letters to you. As you had always been sensitive and caring you seemed to have observed it too. You in fact raised it in some of your letters. I could not tell you anything. I was always praying to God to vindicate me."

During this lengthy intervention, Bayo kept on groaning, shaking and sweating profusely. At times it appeared that he was warding off some enemies unseen by us. He looked like a trapped animal.

When Pero said to Gbade, "Darling, what shall we do to this wretch?" it was Bayo who answered: "All I need is forgiveness and to be allowed to survive. I have more than paid for the harm I did to you. We heard that your husband has been given special power to meet all the exigencies of life and to react to evil. He has embedded in him the traditional spiritual 'boomerang' which has been tormenting me and smashing all those who loved me for almost three decades. I ask both of you to forgive me in the name of God. To err is human, to forgive divine."

Gbade replied, "Go in peace, Bayo. We have forgiven you wholeheartedly. We shall also remember you in our prayers. We shall ask the Almighty Father to forgive you as well."

When the door closed on Bayo, both of us had a feeling of peace and tranquillity. We knew that the angel of discord and all his minions had left our home forever.

"I clung to my husband as I had never done before," Pero related. "I could not help it. I kept on weeping, with tears flowing down my face. All the while Gbade kept on soothing, kissing and cuddling me. I did not know when he piloted me to bed. The next thing I remembered was finding myself in bed the following morning. My wonderful husband was beside me holding my arms. He had such a tender look, full of love on his face."

"You are unblemished; you are spotless; you are stainless; you are indeed worthy, very worthy, to have your 'maiden token' lodged in the Queen's basket," Gbade told her.

After a long pause Gbade continued in whisper, as if talking to himself. "The essence called love can be so soothing, sweet and blissful. Alas, how a gentle twist of fate may expose its harsher side, a sour taste tinged with bitterness and discord. Yet love normally produces an all-pervading fragrance, softness and bliss. Truly blessed indeed is the couple on whom is bestowed from above that all-embracing, all-conquering, enduring true love." …and Gbade's face became suffused with a strange tenderness.

"Darling, you are already dressed up. Are we going out?" asked Pero.

"I have been out and returned," answered Gbade.

"Where from? Why did you not wake me up?"

"You were enjoying your sleep and it would have been wicked to disturb you. Besides, I was preparing a surprise for you," Gbade told her.

"What surprise?"

"Why don't you go into the bathroom and freshen up?" Gbade replied.

Pero, all eagerness, quickly jumped up. When she entered their private sitting room, she could barely believe her eyes. The room had been transformed. A table was set for two. There was a bottle of champagne in the bucket. There were flowers everywhere. There was also a large basket of fruit. In her excitement and wonder she asked, "Where did these come from? What is happening?"

"I went out early to buy them. I wanted to surprise you. "We are celebrating."

"But, dear husband, what is the occasion?" asked Pero.

"With the removal of the horrible barrier between us and the return of true peace to our home, with the removal of the prolonged nightmare, we need to celebrate. All the other members of this household have been told not to disturb us. Come into my arms, dear wife."

Pero threw herself into his arms. After they kissed and hugged he led her to the table. Pero wanted to continue speaking but Gbade said, "No more talking until after our brunch."

After the meal was over, the champagne popped and poured, Gbade said, "Now let us continue our conversation. If you permit, I shall start. How do you feel?" Before she could reply, he added: "I need not ask if you slept well because I know you did."

Pero admitted: "It was my first deep, restful sleep since that fateful night when I was defiled by Bayo. I had really never slept since then. Not only did I sleep last night, I was in heaven."

"Darling, you should have taken me into confidence right from the beginning. Problems shared, especially with a loved one, we are told, reduce the burden." Gbade told her.

"That's easier said than done," countered Pero. She went on: "What respectably married woman would confess to having been raped, especially in our peculiar circumstance? I just could not. I was hoping and praying that, God in his good time would, one day, vindicate me."

"You should have trusted me and confided in me. True love engenders trust." He continued by asking: "And why were you crying on the day you arrived in London?"

Pero replied: "I felt suddenly frightened. I thought that you would discover that night that I had been deflowered. I felt trapped."

"That night after the film on the television, why did you say that you had always been faithful?" asked Gbade.

"The way you looked at me provoked a reply. I was not myself when I blurted out whatever it was I said," replied Pero. "Do you remember the night you related your dream about Bayo to me, how startled I was. The look of fear on my face was all too revealing, was it not? I thought I was going to die. Darling, your understanding of feminine body language is too uncanny. From that day I have been treading with great care and trepidation. I hope I never live through such a situation again." After a time, Pero continued: 'When Bayo, during his confession, referred to the spiritual boomerang embedded in you I was so nervous. I said to myself, 'Could that spiritual boomerang harm me for keeping such a secret from you for so long?'"

"My dear, my ancestors who discovered the secret of such protection would not have been so thoughtless or wicked as to make it harm loved ones. Although we possess this unique power or whatever it is, we still love and protect our loved ones. No harm can come to you through or from me," he told her.

"To be absolutely frank, I am sometimes afraid that

you can read my thoughts. As I previously observed, your understanding of body language and your interpretation of it is frightening," Pero went on.

Gbade intervened, "Sometimes you had a troubled look. Yes, a strange look mixed with pity for me. At such times I became almost certain that you had a well-guarded secret which somehow affected me, a secret which you did not wish unearthed. On such occasions my heart bled for you because I could see that you were under great stress and really sad."

Pero interjected: "Gbade, if you were in my shoes you would feel exactly the same. Often I have asked myself how I could keep such a secret from my husband, a husband who loves me so dearly and whom I also love so much. It was most painful."

To this Gbade said: "When one keeps secrets, the barrier of distrust would always be there. In such a situation it would have been impossible for a couple to live a normal life. One of them would have been living a lie. Supposing Bayo had not come forward to make the confession, what would have happened?"

"My life would have been so miserable. It would be a life of prolonged agony. I would have been living a lie as you rightly put it. Thank God he came. I also thank the

Almighty Father that you really love me and that you are so understanding. I doubt if any other man could have been so accommodating. May God bless you."

"Last night after you went to bed I sat up thinking. I asked myself a lot of questions. One of them was whether not disclosing the rape might have been responsible for the long delay before we had children. Were we being punished because you were not telling the truth?"

"Fancy you saying that," interrupted Pero. "Such a possibility had occurred to me, even before Bayo came. Guilty conscience, I suppose."

Again Gbade intervened: "When I was at the Club last Tuesday I heard of a case almost similar to ours; except that the woman concerned kept on affirming that she was a virgin when she got married, in spite of the facts. She wanted to eat her cake and still have it. Unfortunately for her the truth came out in the end. Her former boyfriend unwittingly let the cat out of the bag. When he became a born again Christian he confessed it to his pastor. Miserable fellow! The pastor turned out to be the brother of the deceived husband. When confronted, in front of her lover, she had to confess. She broke down, cried bitterly and asked for forgiveness.

She, like many others, forgot that to avoid discovery one must not indulge in any misconduct."

"I was afraid that something like that could happen to me." admitted Pero. "Imagine your contempt and the derision." But Gbade quickly observed: "Do you think me capable of holding you in contempt? Can you ever expect derision from me? Never. When we got married, we did so for better or for worse; we became one flesh. You ought to have known me by now. Under no circumstance would I have derided you. If I did so, I would be deriding myself."

"Since we are starting a new life, I suggest that we look at the nature of love afresh," said Gbade.

"I agree entirely."

"A detailed examination of love ought to be made to guide us for the future, if only to strengthen our love," Gbade continued. "Why have we given ourselves so many headaches and heartaches. When I gave you my love you and asked for yours in return, I did not ask whether or not you were a virgin. No! Such a thought never even crossed my mind. I just loved you as you were. I must confess though that at the back of my mind was always the assurance that a girl with your background and education must be a virgin. Love is such a great force – when it comes it exerts so much pressure; when it pulls, the magnetic force is so powerful that you cannot resist. It leaves you no time to wonder or ask questions.

"Love is like a gust of wind, which pushes or drives you into the arms of a loved one, when she or he beckons. Love, the true meaning or import of which is yet to be discovered, is a great driving force. It can push you to great heights. It can make you attain the unattainable. It can make you achieve the seemingly impossible. Love is the all-conquering force. In the words of Paul the Apostle: 'Love is patient. Love is kind. It does not envy. It does not boast. It is not proud. It is not rude. It is not self-seeking. It is not easily angered. It keeps no records of wrongs. Love does not delight in evil, but rejoices with the truth. It always protects, always perseveres. Love never fails.'

"Now Pero, stretch out both hands and clasp mine as we renew our vows. Let us repeat the words of Saint Paul. Let us resolve to follow them for as long as God gives us life. Let our union be a shining example for all those we come in contact with. May God in his mercy grant our prayers." They both chorused 'Amen.'

"Is all forgiven?" asked Pero. "There is nothing to

forgive" answered Gbade.

Thereupon Pero nestled her head on Gbade's chest, and waves of content flowed through the two friends and lovers, now at last truly one.

———◆♥◆———

THE ATONEMENT

How it began

At last, the day for the Annual Anglican Youth Fellowship (AYF) Competition has arrived. As early as five o'clock, long before dawn, I am ready. The buses will leave Obalende bus terminus at seven o'clock prompt. All the AYF members from the various Anglican churches on the island are aware of the arrangements. Normally, walking from St David's church to the terminus takes about twenty minutes. Our house is at the market end of Lewis Street which means an additional ten minute walk. Knowing that I shall linger to watch my favourite squirrels and birds, I set out early.

The usual hustle and bustle of daily life is yet to begin. The road is almost deserted. All is quiet and peaceful. The cool breeze is fresh, clean and soothing – and thanks to the heavy overnight rain, the air is free of dust. Due to the early rains, the elephant grass has grown very tall on both sides of the road. The neatly trimmed hedges are about a foot lower than the elephant grass. The red flowers on the top and sides of the hedges are thick and abundant. The tropical green of the rain-cleansed elephant grass makes a beautiful contrast with the ixora hedges. Behind the tall grass are the flamboyant trees, even taller with their spreading branches covered in yellow flowers.

Sure enough, the grey squirrels are already darting to and fro across the road. The red-eyed turtle doves have already started to twitter, flying from tree to tree; occasionally they touch down looking for seeds and fruits to eat. Watching them is fascinating.

While walking from the church to the police grounds, I see maybe five or six women carrying their wares on their heads going to the market. They sway gracefully as they walk in their multi-coloured dresses. The flower nurseries just beyond the bridge are resplendent with gorgeous flowers and plants. I pause to look at them and at the rockery with the cactuses and African lilies as well as the purple *praecox* that surrounds them. I whisper to myself, "nature is a wonderful artist." The miniature palms interspersed with yucca plants, both *aloifolia* with its mesmerising ivory hue and the light green *rostrala*, looking like bristles of a hedgehog, are stunning. The composite picture is a riot of colour. While I am still admiring this picture of nature in all its glory, the sun peeps out, beaming its light and warmth at me; I feel joyful and I am at peace with myself and the world. Intuition tells me that this will be a special day. I hum a favourite song as I walk along. I then start to think about the day ahead. This will be my first visit to the Posts & Telegraph Institute at Oshodi with its famous picnic sites and playgrounds. I am very keen and hopeful that St David's AYF will win the Archbishop Vining Cup dance competition. Bose and I will represent our branch in the rhumba and waltz as well as the two other steps. We have been practicing daily, working hard at positioning, posture, poise, stance and turns for hours each day for the last three months.

Bose is a dream partner; while I dance, she floats. She excels at all times. It is a delight dancing with her. I hope and pray that Niyi, her excessively jealous boyfriend, will not prevent her from coming to the competition. That would be a disaster. I am still thinking about the enjoyable day ahead as I reach the bus terminus.

I thought that I would be the very first person to arrive, but this is not so. Already standing in front of the first bus are a pair of boys and two girls all wearing the AYF badge. I introduce myself to them as a member from St David's church. They in turn inform me that they belong to the newest AYF branch, from the Trinity Chapel, Alagbon.

Soon the four buses are nearly full, and we start the journey. We stop at various bus stops on the island then four more on the mainland before arriving at Oshodi. We receive a warm welcome from the All Saints branch members who are to be our hosts for the picnic. We are then shown to our bases. Afterwards we are given a half-hour break to look around before we assemble for the devotion. My escort, Bayo, who lives in the neighbourhood, is the current social secretary of All Saints branch. He has used the premises on many occasions so he is able to show me round the compound. Beyond the arena, where the dancing competition is to be held, are the pleasure gardens and playgrounds. The various flower beds and bamboo structures for creeping plants are fantastic. There are different varieties of flowers: hibiscus, buttercup, bachelor's buttons, rose periwinkles, sunflowers, Cana lilies, African lilies and roses of varying colours. The bamboo structures reinforced with steel poles are covered with orange, pink, white and mauve bougainvillea. The garden also contains money plants, morning glory and various kinds of ferns and decorative palms. There are, also, many kinds of trees: Indian Almond, flamboyant, frangipani, and royal palms. There is also a lone Iroko tree, tall, thick and imposing. It looks ancient, dignified and awe-inspiring. It stands in the centre of the landscape like a king – majestic, aloof and magnificent. The half-hour break passes quickly.

The devotion takes place in the open arena enclosed with avocado, grapefruit and orange trees. We sit in a horseshoe formation with the chaplain facing the semi-circle. It is all over in half an hour. Then the elimination contest for the dance competition follows with the judges selecting just six couples to take part in the finals. Bose and I have the highest score. Together with five other pairs, three from the Island and two from the Mainland compete for the coveted cup. I eat lunch very sparingly, mindful of the butterflies in my stomach. The bell summons us, contestants and audience alike, to the main arena. Bose has changed into her flared, pleated lovat skirt to which her white blouse makes a beautiful contrast. She is elegantly poised in the middle of the dance floor as if she is about to soar into the air. I walk briskly to join her. The other five contesting pairs are also in their positions.

Fortunately the contest starts with the rhumba, our favourite step. We dance our hearts out. At one stage it seems as if Bose and I are floating away. At that point the music stops. Bose, the exhibitionist, gives me the nudge; we then give a graceful bow in unison. The applause that follows is long and rapturous, and unsurprisingly we are awarded the highest score of nine. After a short interval, the waltz follows in which Bose and I as well as the couple from All Saints score nine each. But we have the edge as All Saints only scored seven in the rhumba. In the quickstep, thanks to Bose, we score eight with the couple from Ebute-Metta scoring nine; but they still trail behind us as in the previous two steps they scored poorly. In the foxtrot, the last dance, St David's, All Saints and one other pair from the Island score nine each. Bose and I have a total score of 35 and win the competition. All Saints is placed second with 33, and St Peters has 31 in third place. Bose and I receive the coveted Archbishop Vining Cup from the chief judge amidst deafening applause. The impish look in Bose's eyes and her dazzling smile express her pleasure at winning. Bose and I then shake hands with the other two couples. As I shake hands with Temi from All Saints I cannot but notice her hand, which is dainty and extremely soft. My own hand clasps hers for an unduly long time; and as I look into her unique face with its unusually pointed nose and splendidly chiselled chin as well as her twinkling eyes, I become mesmerised.

We both walk slowly away hand in hand towards the barbecue. At first we are both silent; then I break the silence as I introduce myself. "I am Ladi from St David's AYF."

"I am Temi of All Saints AYF. I have a feeling that I have seen you before."

"It's quite possible as I hardly miss any AYF events," I tell her.

On reaching the barbecue spot we deliberately choose a table for two so we can talk together without disturbance. We place our bags to reserve the table and then join the queue for food, with Temi in front so that I can watch her without her noticing. We both receive many congratulations as we choose our food. We then pick our soft drinks and walk back to our table.

My heart is beating fast and I feel dizzy with the thought of being with her. As we sit down we clasp our left hands while picking at our plates with the right hands. I could barely eat as I gaze at her pretty face, her well-rounded cheeks, her pointed nose and chin, her twinkling eyes with their lush eye-lashes, and the crown of abundant hair neatly parted in two in the centre and drawn back into a bun at the back of her well sculptured head. Unlike me, unabashedly examining every inch of Temi's face, she too is examining my face but in a more discreet, ladylike manner. We are both smiling and somewhat quiet. I then suggest we take a walk around the playground. We walk in silence until we reach a cluster of trees and then select a bench beneath them. We sit sideways looking at each other and intuitively we hold hands. The sensation between us is magnetic. The prevailing silence is exceptional. I break the silence saying: "Sweet Temi, a penny for your thoughts."

Temi looks up with a start. "Am I dreaming?" she says quietly.

"Why?" I ask.

"You will not believe it," she answers. "I feel as if we have been transferring our thoughts forwards and backwards, as if in conversation. It would be embarrassing for me to express what I think I heard you say, and my reply!" she adds.

"May I suggest something crazy?"

"Go on, let's have it," she replies with a smile.

I then put my hand into my bag, take out a note pad and tear out two pages, passing one to Temi while keeping the other. "To avoid any embarrassment, let's write out our thoughts and exchange the pieces of paper," I suggest.

"Agreed."

After a short time, I ask Temi if she is ready.

"Yes, ready," she says. We then exchange our pieces of paper.

"Do you mind if I read yours first?" I ask her.

"No; that's fine," she replies.

"What on earth is the matter with me?' I have fallen head over heels in love with him; the feeling I think is mutual."

"Please read out mine."

"It seems that I have fallen in love with her; this is love at first sight. But supposing she does not reciprocate, what will I do? But I am sure she will."

"This is strange," we both say in unison.

Intuitively, we both stand up and embrace. The kiss that follows is passionate and says a lot. We then both sit back gazing into each other's eyes. When I finally break the silence by saying, "I feel so peaceful," Temi answers, "Me too". For the rest of the evening it is as if we are both in a dream. Instead of getting into the bus in which I came, like someone in a trance I follow Temi into her bus that goes to the Yaba terminus. We both sit side by side, in silence and still holding hands. Throughout the bus ride not a word is uttered. When we reach Yaba, Temi leads me to her home on Agard Street. We find her parents in the front yard.

"At last you're back," her mother says.

"We have been anxious," her father adds. "This is why we are sitting here, waiting for you. Who is this young fellow?"

"He is one of our members from St David's Lafiaji," Temi answers. "He and his partner won the cup for St David's. We came a poor second, after all our hard work and practice. All the same I am happy for him. He volunteered to see me home as it is so late."

After commiserating with Temi for not winning the competition, and saying he is sure she'll do better next year, Temi's father turns to me in a friendly manner: "Thank you young man. What's your name?"

"Good evening Sir. Good evening Ma. I am Ladi Adeolu."

"Which Adeolu would that be?" asks the father.

"My father is a civil servant," I answer. "He works at the old secretariat on the Marina."

"Then you must be S.O.'s son!" Temi's father exclaims.

"Yes, I am."

"It's a very small world. He was my immediate boss before his recent transfer on promotion to the Judicial Department. Yes, you look like him. I hope he is well. Please give him our regards."

"Yes sir, I'll do so. I must be on my way. It is getting late."

By way of goodbye, all Temi could manage with her parents present was a squeeze of my hand, but she whispered, "I'll see you in front of the Ambassador at six tomorrow evening." I feel as if I am floating on air as I walk to the bus stop. Throughout the journey all I can think of is Temi. I get down at Beecroft bus stop mechanically. My dreams that night are all of Temi.

Of course we meet again the next day and thus our relationship blossoms. I become a regular visitor to Temi's house and the friendship between her mother and me gets stronger and stronger. And so Temi becomes my life and we are inseparable.

One evening we are seated on a bench in the park

very near Temi's home, one of our favourite meeting places. "I hope you have not forgotten Yeside's birthday party on Saturday evening."

"I have not," Temi replies, "but I won't be able to attend. You remember I told you last week of the death of my aunt back in the village. Mummy thinks that I should accompany her, especially as my Dad will be unable to go. I had to agree as poor Mum never feels at ease going to the village on her own. I am disappointed as Yeside's parties have always been fun. But you go along and enjoy yourself. However, make sure you behave. Don't do anything I wouldn't do."

"As if I would, you naughty girl," is my teasing response.

When I arrive at the party on Saturday, Yeside's guests are already sitting at the tables on the lawn. Yeside takes me round to greet them while introducing me to a few guests that I have never met before. One of them is a very pretty girl, Aduke, who lives in the same compound as Yeside. As there are only three persons at Aduke's table, Yeside suggests that I should join them. In the course of the evening I have a dance with Aduke, who turns out to be a great dancer, almost as good as Bose. We make a handsome pair as we dance.

Although I am enjoying the party, I have the urge to go home to catch up with some revision in preparation for the coming exams.

Aduke also walks home to her family's bungalow about the same time. For the first time Aduke seems to notice the beauty of their garden. She walks very slowly and thoughtfully and tells herself: "This is an excellent compound, well laid out and with lots of flowers and trees." She decides to sit on a bench underneath a tree in front of her home. She carefully selects a spot behind a clump of trees as she does not want anyone to see her. Again she looks round the compound, savouring and admiring the lovely surroundings in which she lives. The neighbourhood is well lit by the full moon. There are so many stars in the sky. The breeze from the Marina is cool and it is indeed a most beautiful night.

Shortly after this, Yeside walks past after seeing Ladi off. She is smiling as if she is sharing Aduke's delightful thoughts. At this point Aduke decides to go inside. She opens the door quietly in order not to disturb her cousin, Tara, and her mother who are already in bed.

Aduke tells her Story

OLABODE OGUNLANA

My head still buzzing from the party, I undress and get ready for bed, but I cannot sleep and nor do I really want to. I just lie on my bed thinking of what took place at Yeside's house. I feel elated. For most of the night I recollect what happened – how I almost swooned when he asked me for a dance. What a dancer! His posture and elegance, his touch, his smile, his charm and his fashionable clothes. He was so sure of himself, and all the girls were dancing around him.

For half of the night I talked to myself. I had hoped that he would ask me for a second dance; but, oh, how selfish of me. He was easily the most admired man at the party and all the girls wanted to dance with him. All too soon he decided to leave. That was a shame.

Did I make the right impression on him? Did he notice me? My heart was pounding all the time when we were together. At last I have found my dream partner, I thought – the one destined for me. There is no doubt that I am in love with him. How I wish that it was already morning. I will ask Yeside all about him.

My thoughts were coming so fast that I could barely breathe. What is happening to me? I asked myself. I felt so excited and happy; but at the same time a little melancholy. I wondered why. And Ladi's image continued to fill my thoughts. His presence seemed to put life into me. I want to be with him every moment of my life, I conclude. But then doubts began to creep in. What chance would I have, what with all those pretty girls buzzing around him? I agonised, before reassuring myself that I am also very attractive, I can hold my own. I shall show them all, I thought. The mere thought of him continued to haunt me. What is this madness that has come over me? There is no doubt about it. I have fallen in love with him. I am no longer in control of myself. May heaven help me. Mercifully, I drift off into sleep at last.

Two mornings after, I am still in a daze. Mum wants to know what is wrong. What can I say? The only answer I can give is, "Nothing, I must be on my way to school". I also avoid my cousin Tara's questioning looks. Later, at school, I could not concentrate during the first two lessons. Even during physical training, which I normally enjoy, I felt listless. I was scolded twice by the games mistress. At break time I keep to myself. It becomes obvious to all the girls that something has happened to me. On the way home, Tolu wants to know what. At first, I would not discuss it but after a lot of coaxing I recount to her my experience of the previous Saturday. Tolu's verdict is: "You are no doubt in love. I have never seen you in this kind of mood. We shall have to find out all about this special boy and see what needs to be done to win him." We both walk on in silence.

After the local cemetery Tolu branches off to go to her own home. When I reach home, only cousin Tara and the maid are in. Mummy is yet to return from her shop. While the maid is getting the meal ready, cousin Tara starts to quiz me. She has been my favourite cousin and constant companion, so I cannot keep anything from her. I recount all that happened at the party the previous Saturday and how I was awake half the night thinking about Ladi. All she said is, "You have been well and truly bitten by the bug. Do be careful. I know that when love comes calling it bites hard. What do you plan to do now?"

"I'll talk to Yeside".

All I could do is to swallow a few mouthfuls of the food on the table before I cross over to Yeside's place. She wants to know if I had enjoyed the party.

"I did, indeed" is my reply. "Since then I have not been myself."

"What do you mean?" asks Yeside.

The words come tumbling out of my mouth. "Who is that young fellow, Ladi? What is his full name? Which school does he attend? How and when can I see him again? Or is he your boyfriend?"

"Take it easy," says Yeside. "Calm down. He is not my boyfriend, at least, not in that way. We belong to the same fellowship in my church. I have known him for many years. He is in the choir, and he sings like an angel; and he dances like a fairy. He is one of the best in the Sunday school. He is also a great debater. His school is very proud of him. He is greatly liked by all, boys and girls. If you are interested in him, as I suspect, I must add that you are too late. He already has a steady girlfriend, an old school friend of mine.

They have been dating for three years."

I felt utterly deflated. I flop into a chair. What a disaster! What is going to happen to me? I feel numb. Suddenly, I feel faint. In fact, I must have passed out. The next thing I remember is Yeside patting me on the back and rubbing my arms. Then she sits beside me, rocking me to and fro. I become blank. After some time I hear myself speaking, "Where am I? What happened?"

"I'll walk you home," Yeside says. I am without feeling whatsoever. How I got back home I do not know.

We enter by the front door and Tara is in the living room, all by herself. She quickly jumps up on seeing us. "What happened? You are looking so pale, Aduke. Yeside, what is the matter?" she asks. They whisper together and then both of them pilot me to my bedroom. My shoes are removed. Cousin Tara goes out and brings some tablets. She passes to me a glass of water and asks me to take the tablets. I must have fallen asleep. When I eventually awake, both Mummy and Tara are with me. "If you do not feel like talking now, don't," says Mummy. "Just rest. Rest your head on my lap." She then starts to rock me like a baby. Very soon I am asleep again. Later that night another cousin, a doctor, enters with a nurse. He examines me thoroughly. With persuasion I take some broth and a slice of bread. I then go back to my bed and sleep.

The next morning I feel a lot better. Cousin Tara is with me. She is looking at me with some anxiety. Then Mother comes in. "My daughter, my baby," she exclaims. "Do not worry. There are many young men around. Ladi is not the only man in the world. Someone else will come for you." But the mere mention of the name, Ladi, puts new life into me. I could only murmur. "It's Ladi I want," I insist. "No other man. I must have him. I cannot love another." I see mother and Tara exchanging looks.

A few days later, I make a further plea to Yeside to arrange another meeting with Ladi. It will afford me an opportunity to plead my case. Yeside refuses bluntly. "Did I not tell you my past relationship with Temi? She was not just a classmate; we were childhood friends. What sort of friend would she think I am to hear that I have been conspiring with you to pinch her boyfriend. Look for help elsewhere."

Yeside's refusal to help me whips up my resolve to do everything possible to avenge my imagined grievance against Temi. "She it was who pinched the man intended for me by providence," I persuade myself. From then on I start collecting all the available information about Temi. In particular, I look for evidence that she is double-dating with a view to using such information to discredit her in Ladi's eyes.

One evening my mother asks me to deliver a parcel to one of her friends. It turns out to be a lucky evening for me. As I approach the address I see Ladi coming out from a nearby house heading in my direction. I quicken my pace so I can speak to him. Fortunately I am very smartly dressed. Switching on what I hoped to be a bewitching and dazzling smile, I say: "Ladi, I haven't seen you since Yeside's party. I hope all is well with you. I am on my way to see your neighbour. Do you mind walking with me." As charming as ever, Ladi replies, "That will be a great pleasure and it's on my way. Good to see you too."

We walk along together. I tell Ladi all about myself. As we approach the house of my mother's friend, I take a bold step. I again refer to Yeside's party expressing how I enjoyed Ladi's company. "I feel as if I had known you all my life. I would like us to be good friends," I tell him. "Why not?" Ladi replies," especially as we are both friends of Yeside."

We part on a friendly note. On a few occasions I contrive to have other 'accidental' meetings with Ladi. On the last of such occasions I told Ladi that when I told Yeside about our friendship she had told me that "Ladi and Temi are inseparable". Ladi confirms that he and Temi have made an irrevocable commitment to each other. He adds that he cannot love anyone else. I was determined to have the last word and said mischievously and seemingly jocularly, "I have noted your commitment and devotion to Temi. However, should Temi at any time disappoint you, please remember that you have Aduke waiting in the wings." Although the tone sounded playful, the message was intended to be serious. In my self-delusion, I feel that I am making progress in winning Ladi's heart.

The following day I discuss the matter with my friend, Tolu. During the discussion Tolu tells me that years back, as children at primary school, Temi, who was then living with her married elder sister, had stayed in the same compound with her, with her elder brother, Debo, and an older sister, Bibayo. Tolu also disclosed that her elder brother Debo was keen on Temi. He had in fact approached her a year earlier try to renew their old childhood friendship. At that time Temi had told Debo that Ladi was her only love. Similarly, when I seek the advice of school friends – Teju, Tolu, Tola and Ronke on the strategy I need to get Ladi to switch his affections and drop Temi in my favour, the girls talk of possible plans. However, I decide to take action to get a rapid result: I cook up a devilish plan. I ask for Tara's assistance. Tara and Gbenga, Ladi's elder brother, had been in a relationship for some time. At my request Tara is to send Gbenga a letter that will require an urgent reply. The urgent reply for delivery to Tara will be sent through Ladi on his way back from school, as Ladi's school and the compound where Tara and I live are on the same road.

My plan is to feign illness at school and return to the house to await Ladi's visit to Tara. I know that Tara, my mother and the maid will all be away from home at that time. Indeed almost the entire compound with its six bungalows will be virtually deserted at that time of the day; that will make the coast clear for me to put my plan into action. Tara agreed, and the next day at school after complaining of a bad - but faked - stomach ache and headache I am sent to the sick-bay. After a while I say I am feeling better and the nursing sister sends me home. Two hours later, Ladi knocks on the door. It is me, and not Tara, who greets him. I have a large towel wrapped around me and say with a sweet smile: "Sorry Ladi, that you had to knock twice. I was in the shower. I was getting ready to go out, but I had promised cousin Tara to delay my outing in order to collect her letter."

As we were about to enter the living room, my bath towel – as a result of my manipulation - slips off me; and conveniently very near the sofa. At that moment my back is towards Ladi. I then turn to face him, saying, "Oops, please forgive me Ladi, how clumsy."

While pretending to struggle to replace my bath wrap I go towards my bedroom but hesitate at the door and say: "Did you not like what you saw?"

"I am not here to watch a nude display," Ladi retorted. "I am a very busy person and I have no time to waste. I shall leave Tara's letter on the sofa and shut the door on my way out." He was clearly shaken and disgusted.

"Please do not leave in such a great haste. I shall be out in a jiffy," I implore him from behind the door. Hastily putting on a very smart frock, I return to him and kneeling say, "Please forgive me, I did not mean to embarrass you."

"You just did. Please get up and sit on a chair," Ladi instructs me. "Supposing Tara or someone else comes in now, what would such a person think."

"Am I forgiven? Then give me a hug, I shall never offend again," I continue in a seductive tone.

"I will do no such thing," he replied angrily, "what do you think you are doing; behaving like a depraved person."

"I am just showing you how much I love you, Ladi," I blurt out.

"No decent and well brought up girl shows love in such a crude way,. Stop behaving so badly." Ladi's face was dark with fury.

"Please Ladi, my overwhelming love for you is killing me. Please accept me; I shall be your slave. I shall do anything. Just say you like me. I will have no objection if you just have me and discard me afterwards. I shall be content. I promise to be at your beck and call at any time," I plead, but with no effect.

"You are disgusting," replied Ladi.

He then walked out leaving me alone to mull over what had just happened. "Mr High and Mighty," I say quietly, as my own anger rises. "You have not heard the end of this matter. You will yet have me or pay for your refusal."

At school, Aduke informs her four friends that she no longer has any interest in Ladi. In a tone seemingly full of relief, she tells them: "He is not a man; he is impotent." Her friends look at her in horror. Pressed to tell all, she relates a slanted account of what happened. One of Aduke's friends makes the observation, "How could a girl so ill yesterday have found the strength and inclination for such a performance."

Promptly Aduke replies, "My illness yesterday was feigned. You no longer need to crack your heads working out a strategy."

"This is a case of sour grapes," taunts another of her friends.

"No, I am dead serious" Aduke counters. Tolu makes the observation that the break period will be over in three minutes and suggests that they wait behind after school to discuss the issue fully.

The five friends have a serious debate when they meet again after school. Teju starts off. She tells me off for having devised such a reckless, shameful and foolish plan, just to snare a boy who is obviously well brought up and who would not dream of involving himself in any form of immoral behaviour. She adds that Aduke has let the group down and should be ashamed of herself; and she made other scathing comments. Aduke maintains that she is right in her assumption and points out that her beauty and her well-proportioned body, as well as her willingness to accept a casual relationship with Ladi, ought to have done the trick. "He must be impotent. No normal male would stand there and react, or rather not react, to my advances as Ladi did."

Tolu, Aduke's best friend, naturally takes her side, saying: "From what Aduke and I have discovered, Ladi would not have hesitated to have Aduke, unless Aduke's accusations are true and he really is impotent." She agrees with Aduke that she should close Ladi's file, forget all about him and find another worthy boyfriend.

Ronke cautions the group, especially Aduke. She advises: "An issue such as the one confronting us cannot be discussed in a casual manner nor considered lightly; there are so many sides to the issue that ought to be given very careful examination." She adds that she had on many occasions met Ladi, who struck her as being sincere and open. The impression she got was that Ladi is someone worthy of trust and respect. "I would expect such a person to rebuff you as he rightly did," Ronke told Aduke. "You deserve what you got; you are envious of what Temi and Ladi have going for them."

Tola made no remark but wore a thoughtful look on her face.

Tolu and Aduke were well aware, all along, that Ronke knew Temi. Aduke had hoped that this discussion would be fully reported to Temi by Ronke, and that Temi would send Ladi packing. Indeed, this was partly the motive for Aduke's underhand plan. For her own part, Tolu thought to herself that Ladi's dismissal would leave the coast clear for Debo, her brother. It was all a sordid conspiracy, such as only the 'saucy five' (as Aduke and her group of school friends were known) would indulge in.

As expected, Tolu reported these developments to Debo and urged him to try his luck again. But she advised him to wait for about two weeks or so before making any move. This was to leave room for Ronke to report the discussion to Temi. Ronke, out of loyalty to her friend, duly did this. She cautioned her to be extremely careful and circumspect in handling the matter, while making the observation that, from the little she knows of Ladi, he appears to be a decent and reliable young man. "I also know that you love him very much. These are good enough reasons for handling the issue delicately and carefully." Temi should not leave herself in a position to be the loser, whatever happens.

She concludes by asking Temi a hypothetical question. "If it's true that he's impotent what will you do?"

"Nothing short of actually making love with him can prove or disprove that," answered Temi, "and I cannot allow any man, no matter how much I love him, to make love to me until after he has married me. To do otherwise would mean disregarding all that my upbringing has taught me. Besides, it is against our traditions and culture."

"What do you intend to do about it?" asks Ronke.

"Let's wait and see," Temi replies. "Matters will sort themselves out."

"As we were talking, what you said some time ago struck me," says Ronke.

"What was that?"

"You complained about the number of girls dancing around Ladi, especially two in particular," Ronke answers. "Supposing he makes love to one of them and she becomes pregnant, where will that leave you?"

"How can an impotent boy impregnate a girl?" answers Temi contemptuously. Speaking more seriously Temi adds: "With time things will sort themselves out."

Temi's Drastic Actions

Poor Temi is restless and sleepless that night. Her long , deep meditation ends on a sad note. "Either way I shall lose out. He may sleep with one of the two girls, or even both of them. What if they become pregnant? The only option is to wait, by that I mean that the

195

wedding I had long planned will either have to be put off indefinitely or I shall get stuck with an impotent man, who will then be no man. In the name of God, what would I do? I know what I will do. I shall use the opportunity to call Ladi's attention to his two special admirers and all the other girls. I shall tell him that I do not have the stamina or inclination to fight any rival in the name of love. I shall tell him that our relationship has to be broken off so that I can have peace of mind. After watching for a brief period I will know if he truly loves me and me alone. God will also reveal whether or not he is really a complete man. It will, however, break my heart to call off the relationship, such a sweet relationship. May heaven help me." She has a rough and sleepless night.

The following evening Ladi shows up as usual. Temi's behaviour is peculiar. As he is leaving, Temi informs him that she has decided that in view of his many female admirers, their relationship should be broken off. She stresses that she is serious and Ladi is not to visit her again. Ladi is stunned and shocked. To stop herself from crying Temi quickly turns round and runs into the house. Ladi remains rooted to the spot for some time; then he leaves in bewilderment.

It is another sleepless night for Temi. "What on earth have I done? I hope that I have not lost the man I truly and deeply love. This game of love is both mad and dangerous," she thinks to herself. Similarly, Ladi could not sleep. All sorts of thoughts run through his mind. He feels numb and half dead. The following three weeks are bleak and sad. Pride prevents him from calling on Temi to beg her to reconsider her decision. He is, in addition, deeply hurt especially as he has previously told Temi that there was no truth in the allegations.

One evening, returning from an outing, Temi is accosted by Debo. Temi reminds him that she had previously informed him that she already has a steady boyfriend. Debo replies that he has decided to have another try as "old friends are better than new; besides, the situation might have changed."

"No, it has not changed," Temi replies. Then Debo starts calling on her daily, pleading to be given a chance. Temi points out that it is impossible for a girl to love two boys at the same time. Debo, however, persists. He then brings a card inviting Temi to a literary event. Out of boredom and to soothe her jaded nerves - as well as to teach Ladi a lesson - she accepts. Debo interprets this to be an act of capitulation on the part of Temi.

He decides to exploit the situation. As he takes up the old tale, Temi with her jaded nerves blurts out that she does not love him. "I already have a steady boyfriend with whom I am deeply in love. Please keep away from me," she ends in exasperation.

Back home, a very troubled Temi sits on her favourite bench beneath the Indian Almond tree, thinking and fretting. She has not seen Ladi for three weeks. If only he would come I shall be rescued from the unwanted attentions of suitors like Debo. She is silently asking: "Has Ladi lost interest?" forgetting that it was she who asked him to stop coming. She becomes even more restless and troubled. Although she does not wish to discuss her problem with anyone, it is so obvious, even to her, that she needs advice, and urgently, otherwise she may go crazy. At the same time she does not wish to relent or pay Ladi a visit. She is truly in a dilemma.

For quite some time, Auntie Agnes, a tutor living in the same compound with Temi, has been watching her. Temi's usual smiles have vanished. Once a singing nightingale, she has now lost her voice. Auntie Agnes has come to the conclusion that something must be wrong. "At the risk of being called a nosey-parker, I shall speak to her," she concludes. In any case

Auntie Agnes has in the past taken a keen interest in her, especially in her studies. Seeing Temi sitting on the bench with a forlorn look she approaches her and says: "Temi, I have noticed your attitude and demeanour lately. They are so unlike the Temi we all know. Do you have some problems? You never know, I may be able to help. You no longer smile or sing. You are less sociable, locking yourself up in your room on the pretext that you are studying. Besides, I have not seen your Ladi around for some time. What is the problem? Please take me into your confidence."

Temi sighs before replying. "I do have a problem, but I would rather not bother you." Pressed by Auntie Agnes, she explains that she had asked Ladi not to come again, but living without him is proving difficult. "It has not been easy. I have been going through hell," she explains in a broken voice.

"Why did you send Ladi away?" asks Auntie Agnes. "He has too many female admirers, they dance round him all the time. The rumour is that he is romantically linked with two of them," replies Temi.

"Did you confront him with these accusations? If so, what was his explanation?"

"He said that they were not true and that I am his

only love."

"Obviously, you did not believe him," Auntie Agnes persists. "Why not? True love always trusts."

Temi hesitates but decides against telling Auntie Agnes about the matter of impotence. "You cannot go on like this," Auntie Agnes advises. "What do you plan to do? Why don't you send for him if you cannot go to him yourself," she suggests.

"I cannot. I cannot eat my words."

"You made a mistake by acting on unproved accusations. Own up and accept your mistake. Do not stress yourself unnecessarily," concludes Auntie Agnes, before taking her leave.

Temi, dejected and worried, continues to ponder what to do. Her thoughts are interrupted by her young cousin, Sola. "Auntie Temi, I have been looking for you all over the place. I have been standing here for quite some time without your noticing me. What is it? Can you spare a few minutes? I want to speak to you,"

"Yes, sit down," Temi says.

"I have not seen Uncle Ladi here for some time," Sola tells her. "I hope he is quite well. I had meant to go to the island in search of him; but I thought I'd talk to you first before doing so." Before Temi could answer, he continues. "Besides, I have seen that hungry looking boy who comes asking for you. He has been here two or three times. I saw you with him the other day near the football field. Don't tell me you want to replace Uncle Ladi with him."

Embarrassed by Sola's comment and jolted out of her inertia, Temi thinks this maybe a good chance to extricate herself. Sola had thought that Auntie Temi would flare up but instead she says, "I want you to do me a favour, Sola. I want you to go immediately to Ladi's place. Tell him that Auntie Temi is dying to see him. Please do not say I sent you. Go without delay."

Sola immediately runs as fast as he can to the bus terminus. When the visitor comes in Ladi cannot believe it: it is Sola, Temi's young cousin. Ladi hardly knows what to think, but after hearing what Sola has to say he hugs Sola and tells him that he will come over to the mainland later in the evening.

Ladi goes out of his way to look as smart and presentable as he can. Unknown to him Temi is doing exactly the same thing. With her hair neatly brushed and caught into a bun at the back, she sits demurely beneath her favourite tree, pretending to be reading a novel. Every so often, she looks towards the main gate. The moment the gate opens she jumps up and runs to meet Ladi. They fall into each other's arms with tears of joy running down their cheeks. Barely able to speak, Temi leads Ladi to the bench on which she has been sitting.

Unbeknown to the two lovers, Auntie Agnes and Sola are watching from one of the windows on the top floor. Looking at each other they both smile, smiles of happiness and contentment at having helped the two lovers to be reconciled. Still holding hands, Temi tells Ladi just how sad she has been, feeling almost suicidal. "I missed you so much. I was forever blaming myself for sending you away."

Ladi consoles her while confessing that he too had been despondent. "When Sola came to see me, my heart started pounding. After telling me that you wanted to see me again, I hugged him for bringing the news that I had been praying to hear. May God bless him for being the bearer of such good news. Now here we are together once again. It has been a nightmare; a very bad dream."

Temi wants to know what has been happening to Ladi. "I suppose that my two rivals have been dancing for joy in the hope that the coast was clear for them," she whispers.

"How can you utter such words? Ladi asks. "It has been a very sad experience. Whenever I got back from school I locked myself in my room to study, but could barely read a word for thinking of you. I felt very ashamed. How would I face the world? It is not funny for a popular young man like me, the head boy of my school, to have been dropped by his girlfriend? I could have never lived it down. It would have hounded me for the rest of my life. I had once sworn to myself that if any girl were to break off a relationship with me, I would never make up with her. Look at me now though, racing back to you. I suppose that you and your friends would have been laughing at me behind my back, saying that the almighty Ladi had been cut down to size. I should perpetually hang my head down in shame."

"What are you talking about," Temi interposes. "I am the one who crawled back. Sola came to you at my request. With all the pain and heart-ache, I had to come off my high horse. I could not afford to lose you. I missed you terribly. It has been a great ordeal."

"Never mind," says Ladi, embracing her fondly. "Let us put the bad dream behind us. Let us march on into a good and joyous future. As if all I was going through was not bad enough, Aduke came along and offered her shoulders for me to cry on. The cheek of it!"

"Same here, Debo came several times saying that he heard that the situation had changed and that I needed someone to look after me," says Temi. "Of course he was sent packing."

When Ladi eventually gets up to leave for home, she sees him off intending to accompany him as far as the football field; but instead she ends up at the bus terminus. As a result Ladi has to accompany her back home. At last she says, "Good night my love. When shall I see you tomorrow?"

"I shall be a bit late because I have to see the doctor tomorrow" replies Ladi.

"I hope it's nothing serious," Temi inquires. "No, it's just that my prospective employer wants a medical report as part of their procedure before I start the job. They want me to start work on Monday immediately after the exams."

The following day, on his way back from the doctor whose surgery is on the mainland, Ladi calls at Temi's home. "How did it go?" she asks.

"It all went well. As I previously told you, it's the routine medical examination for new entrants. The original copy of the report will be sent to my prospective employers direct. I have been given this copy for my records.".

"May I read it?" Temi asks, excitedly. The envelope is handed to her. She reads it carefully and slowly. Huge relief shows on her face as she reads the doctors remark that "the applicant is a very healthy young man without any deformity or abnormality."

Thus the two lovers resume their courtship. With this new beginning their love grows stronger. It seems all too soon when, seven years after Ladi and Temilade first met at the AYF picnic, their formal engagement and marriage ceremony takes place in a whirl just before Ladi travels to London for further studies. It is fully eighteen months later when Temi joins him. After four years in London, they return home to Nigeria together.

* * *

After the five friends – Aduke, Tola, Tolu, Teju and Ronke – finished at High School only the last three keep in close touch with one another. Aduke stays aloof from her former friends most of the time, though she gets in touch with them occasionally. As always, she is constantly scheming and planning some fresh devilry. Following her offer of a shoulder for Ladi to cry on, which was firmly rebuffed, she starts to watch the movements of Ladi and Temi. She vows to take revenge on both of them - on Ladi, the heartless creature who spurned her love, and on Temi who in her fertile imagination remained the snatcher of the man intended for her by providence. She continues to spy on Ladi and Temi by setting up an elaborate network of informants to monitor their movements both at home and in London.

Pursuing her latest plans Aduke decides to pay a visit to London, taking the opportunity to make some business contacts. Whilst in London she telephones Tinuke, her mother's first cousin. Tinuke was married many years ago to a Swiss national who had lived in West Africa for years. Both of them had decided to retire and live in Zurich. Tinuke has one daughter, Otolorin, generally known as Oto. As Tinuke would like her daughter to marry a Nigerian, she broaches the subject with Aduke. Aduke responds positively to this proposition and promises to look after Oto and be her guardian when she comes to Lagos. Soon afterwards,

Aduke returns to Nigeria and is pleased to receive a letter from Tinuke with the news that Oto would soon arrive in Lagos. From the accompanying photograph of Oto, the little girl Aduke had previously seen about twenty years before, has grown into a very pretty young lady. At last Aduke will have a companion, like a younger sister, to live with her. Before Oto's arrival Aduke commissions an interior decorator to look at the bedroom and the adjoining lounge that she has in mind for Oto's use. She is determined to make her feel at home. Oto will be the key to a plan she is hatching.

At last, Oto arrives. Aduke is delighted and even the maid is surprised to see her in such a good mood. As Oto appears in the airport terminal, Aduke greets her: "My dear child, you have grown into a beauty. I am delighted to have you stay with me. I hope you will like it here." Later, with Oto's suitcases in the boot of the car, they drive into the city making light conversation. Oto comments on the development of Lagos with all the new skyscrapers. Reaching Aduke's home, Oto is impressed by the apartment and after unpacking her bags she and Aduke share a meal and continue their conversation. "Your mother's letter says that you are a very competent secretary with working knowledge of English, French and German. How did you come to learn French and German?" Aduke asks.

Oto points out that having schooled in Zurich she learnt to speak and write the two languages reasonably well. "Auntie, have you started looking around for a suitable opening for me?" Aduke replies that she has, and an advertisement in that day's paper may prove suitable. After reading the advert, Oto agrees that the job advertised may be just right for her. "It reads as if it has me in mind." She prepares her c.v. and application letter the following morning which Aduke's driver delivers to the address indicated. A week later Oto is invited for a test and interview. The evening before the interview Aduke has a long talk with Oto. She ends by saying, "Please dress modestly and with care. Use minimal makeup. It is crucial you get this position as secretary to the new manager. When you do I shall advise you further on what you should do."

After the test and first interview, Oto and two others are short-listed for the personnel manager's final interview. After that interview, Oto's papers and those of the other short-listed applicants are passed to the manager. They are asked to report the following day. Aduke gives Oto another pep talk. "So far so good," she tells Oto. "I have selected a very pretty but formal dress for you. I must compliment you on your dress sense. This frock is the type a good and sensible manager will appreciate. The dress is your opening gambit, so to speak, and first impressions count. When you are presented to the young manager, be respectful and courteous without being subservient. Relax and feel at home. Exude all the charm and confidence you can. You cannot fail to succeed. I want you to capture and captivate him from the very start."

"Why all this fuss, Auntie," asks Oto. "If I am finally selected I shall only be the manager's secretary, not his wife or mistress. Auntie, you are purring like a cat. You look so excited. What exactly is happening?" But Aduke just ignores her and continues with her instructions. "You must be on your best behaviour, demure, correct and proper. I am sure that you will get the job. When you are eventually appointed you must be diligent. Your conduct must be exemplary. With your looks, all the men will be wanting to get to know you. Please do not flirt with any of them. Concentrate on your work and on pleasing the manager. He's the one who must fall for you. If you follow all my instructions, you will within a few months have him eating out of the palm of your hand."

Oto is shocked at Auntie Aduke's scheming, and begins to wonder if there is a secret motive for her aunt's interest. The next day Oto returns to the house at lunchtime and tells Aduke that she has been given the job. She shows her the letter of appointment and Aduke is delighted. "Congratulations, my dear. This is just the beginning," she comments. "When you assume your duties next Monday, make yourself indispensable. Make the manager dependent on you for his continued success."

Oto is astounded. She asks Aduke: "Auntie, what are we talking about? The position of secretary or something else?"

"At the appropriate time I shall explain" is Aduke's cryptic answer. When Oto starts the new job, she follows Aduke's instructions to the letter. As predicted by Aduke, she captivates everyone in the establishment, including the manager, proving herself punctual and very efficient.

The manager travels a lot. Whenever he returns, reports have to be prepared, and this means that Oto often has to work late. The manager is a well-mannered and polished man, and always very proper in his dealings with Oto. He sees Oto not just as a personal assistant but as a young sister. Even Temi, the manager's wife, respects her. As a result, both of them treat Oto as a member of their family.

One evening, Aduke confides in Oto about what she refers to as her previous relationship with Ladi, Oto's boss. Of course, she gives her a twisted version of what really happened. According to her, Ladi was her boyfriend and they were very much in love. Everything was going well until Temi came along and stole him from her. She had been waiting for an opportunity to take her revenge; and now is the time. For extra effect, Aduke resorts to crocodile tears as she relates her story, in order to gain Oto's sympathy. She urges Oto to be particularly nice to Ladi so that he can be enticed into an affair that will drive a wedge between Temi and him.

Aduke's convincing acting persuades Oto to go along with her Aunt's plan. She starts to make subtle advances to her boss. On one occasion Ladi calls attention to a rare lapse and asks what has come over her. "Until recently you have been a perfect secretary," Ladi tells her. "You dressed modestly and your manners, demeanour and work were first class. But in the last week or so something has come over you. Look at your dress, it is outrageous! What is the matter? Do you have any problems? Unless you change and become your old self I will have to replace you." Oto is contrite and apologises. Before long, however, she relapses. Ladi has to remind her that their relationship should remain strictly that of employer and employee. The irony of the situation is that Oto has actually fallen for Ladi, and now there is no way that she can bring herself to harm him. She tells Aduke about her feelings and how she now regrets being part of the conspiracy to destroy Ladi and Temi's marriage.

Shortly after explaining the situation to Aduke, she resigns her appointment, packs her belongings and returns to her parents in Zurich. Aduke sees Oto's conduct as a betrayal and becomes even more bitter and frustrated. Her previous love for Ladi has turned into a vitriolic hatred; she is determined to do anything to harm Ladi and Temi. Totally obsessed with Ladi, she refuses to consider marriage. Instead she throws herself into her business, intent on making serious money to entice Ladi, if only to spite Temi.

Aduke refuses several marriage proposals until, after pressure from her ageing mother, she marries a man fifteen years older than herself. It is a most unhappy marriage but as far as Aduke is concerned, the marriage is to kill time until such time as she can be in a position to take over Ladi and inflict her revenge. Her husband is wealthy, and when he suddenly dies he leaves Aduke a rich widow. The union of wealth and wickedness breeds disaster. Aduke's unhappy marriage produced a son, Folarin, the image of his father. He in turn gets married to Feyi, a young, clever, pretty lady from a good but impoverished family. True to form, Aduke makes Feyi's life very difficult. Aduke's daughter-in-law is an engineer with a promising future but her mother-in-law insists she becomes her personal assistant in the trading business.

Out of frustration, the young couple leave Nigeria for South Africa where they have a child. One day the child becomes ill and is taken to hospital where it is discovered that she has a very rare blood disease. The best treatment for the disease can only be given by a specialist at an expensive hospital. As the cost of the treatment is above their means, they lose hope. However, in the hospital Feyi meets a fellow Nigerian, a Mrs. Oye, who visits them in their home and learns of Feyi and Folarin's predicament. Later, the Nigerian lady tells her husband, an engineer, all about Feyi's child and the help needed for her treatment. A few days after, the couple pay another visit to Feyi and inform her that a deposit has been made to the specialist hospital for the child's treatment. After three months treatment, the child's health improves and the kindness brings the two families closer.

Aduke is very unhappy and lonely despite her great wealth. Her frustration worsens daily. Alone and unloved, she starts to miss her son and his family. Out of desperation she decides to pay them a visit. She is pleasantly surprised at the very warm welcome she is given by her son and daughter-in-law. In due course she learns about the generosity and kindness of the Oyes. One evening Folarin and Feyi invite the Oyes and their parents to dinner, since Aduke had expressed the wish to meet and personally thank them for being so good and generous to her son and his family.

Aduke is stunned to discover that her daughter-in-law's benefactors are in fact Ladi and Temi, her arch enemies, who had moved to South Africa. At first she is dumb and taciturn; but gradually she thaws as Ladi and Temi engage her and the others in conversation. In the end they all manage to have a fairly pleasant evening together and Aduke becomes warmer towards the visitors. After Ladi and Temi leave, Feyi who is naturally observant asks her mother-in-law if she had previously met Ladi and Temi. Aduke says she had briefly met them several years ago without going into details.

Soon afterwards she retires to her room. It is only natural that Aduke should be moved. All her life she has been envious of Ladi and Temi. She has done her best to harm them as well as to destroy their happy marriage. In return they have repaid her wickedness and hatred with the kindness and generosity shown towards her son's family and especially to her granddaughter. But for them, the family might have lost the child. Aduke is overcome by remorse. For the best part of that night she reviews her life, past and present. She realises how wicked she has been. What she thought of as a love affair she now clearly realises was just unreciprocated love. Whereas she fell head over heels in love with Ladi, he had never at any time returned the love nor did he try to convey such an impression. She had been a victim of self-delusion. Whilst agreeing that she is envious of the healthy relationship between Ladi and Temi, she also agrees that her hatred of them over the years has no basis or justification. She is struck by remorse. She resolves to confess her misdeeds and sins to Ladi and Temi. Not only would she ask for their forgiveness she would seek advice on how to atone for her sins. It is a completely different Aduke who wakes up in the morning.

Later that afternoon Aduke asks Feyi to telephone Temi. Aduke's explanation is that she wishes to thank them for the visit as well as for their kindness towards her daughter-in-law and her granddaughter. Not only is she very friendly over the telephone but she arranges a meeting with them for the next day. She goes on her own to see Ladi and Temi and is warmly received by both of them. After tea she announces the purpose of her visit. In an impassioned speech she expresses her sorrow and apologies: "Ladi and Temi, I am here to offer unreserved apologies for my wickedness and all the harm I have done to you. I am full of remorse. I want to confess my other misdeeds, those that you do not even know about. I am hoping that after I have made a full confession you will find it in your hearts to forgive me. I am sure that God will show me what I need to do to atone for my sins."

When Ladi gestures to be allowed to reply, Aduke

asks him to hear her out. "I am eager to get it all off my chest. After that I shall listen to what you and Temi may have to say. I thank you greatly for the mercy and kindness you showed to those you thought were total strangers. From what I have been told by my son and daughter-in-law, I believe that you would have acted in the same way even if you had known who the child's grandmother was. I also wish to express my appreciation for the way you received me yesterday, even after you knew my relationship with Feyi and her daughter. To my shame I have to confess the other evils I had done against you. You remember the dream flat in Golders Green in London you very much liked and wanted to rent and how it all fell through at the last moment. I caused that. I got to know about it from Zacc, my boyfriend, and asked him not to let it to you. On your return to Nigeria I planted Dele, your steward, in your household. Your precious medication, the hormone treatment from France that got missing was thrown away by him on my instructions. The many accidents in the home you had during his stay with you were contrived by me. The worst was that I planted Oto in your office, Ladi. My plan was for her to seduce you and to ruin your marriage.

" I am really ashamed of myself. When I get back to Lagos I shall see my priest and seek his advice on how best I can atone for my many sins. While I have been going steadily downhill, both of you have been rising higher. I was consorting with and learning from the devil; whereas all the time you had made the fear of God your watchword. Now I have seen the error of my ways. I have destroyed myself through envy, frustration, hatred and the pursuit of revenge. I ruined myself for the sake of what I thought was love; it was self-delusion. Please forgive me and may God have mercy on me. I must leave now; please do not tell Folarin and Feyi what I have told you. May God bless you for keeping my confession secret. Again, thank you for your kindness to my family, especially my granddaughter. Who knows, but for your timely assistance she might have died."

Ladi's brief reply was, "Aduke, we feel really sorry for you," adding "We shall always remember you in our prayers. God will help you turn a new leaf. We harbour no resentment or animosity against you. The Almighty Father will forgive you. May His mercy rest and abide with all of us."

After returning to Lagos, Aduke loses no time to

visit her priest. She confesses to him: "I have offended against the heavenly Father and my neighbours. I have sinned. I wish to make atonement. I have come so that you can pray for me, advise and point me in the right direction towards making the atonement." She recounts everything from the beginning to the end and then the priest prays for her. He then asks if she has any specific idea in mind for her atonement. She answers that she had thought of volunteering her time to charity, working at a home for blind, disabled, or deaf and dumb people; or at an orphanage or an institute for the homeless or destitute. She was willing to give financial support to any charity the church might advise. After a short pause, her priest informs her about a new home that caters for troubled girls. Among other things the girls learn trades and homecraft at the institution with the intention of giving them a positive role in society. Although the home works under the supervision of the Diocese, it is privately financed. Aduke immediately expresses her interest in this home, remembering that she was once a troubled girl herself. She thinks to herself: "If these girls can be prevented from making the same mistakes that I made, then that is a duty I must perform." The priest then gives her a letter of introduction to Mother Olga Mary, the director of the girls' home.

Arriving at the girls' home the next day, she is asked to wait a few minutes for Mother Olga Mary, and while waiting she browses through several Christian magazines and literature on the racks and tables. While waiting she recalls her school days and especially her friends, Tolu, Teju, Tola and Ronke. She wonders what has become of them. She becomes engrossed in her own thoughts when Mother Olga Mary arrives.

"Good morning, I am Mother Olga Mary. What can I do for you?" In response Aduke hands her the letter of introduction. After reading the letter Mother Olga Mary invites Aduke into her office. On sitting down Aduke is taken aback when the Mother says, "Aduke it has been a long time. What has been happening to you? You do not look your usual self although it has been ages since we last met." Surprised, Aduke answers, "Mother have you mistaken me for someone else? I don't remember that we have ever met."

"Really" replies Mother Mary "Think back and remember your school days. Do you remember the band of five, 'the saucy five' of which you were the undisputed leader."

"Of course I do, but how would you know about them."

"Well, I should know about them because I was one of them. Do you remember the shy one who spoke only when necessary?"

With this she stares hard at Mother Mary. Suddenly she exclaims: "My goodness, Tola. What a pleasant surprise!" Mother Olga Mary responds saying, "Yes, it's me. Now, tell me your story. I understand that you are a very successful business woman and very wealthy. Why on earth, with all of that, would you want to serve in this home and work without pay?"

"It's a long story."

"Let's talk about it," says Mother Olga Mary, adding, "I am so pleased to see you after all these years but I have never seen you before in such a sombre mood. It's quite a turn around. Fancy, the usually gay and mischievous Aduke. It's unbelievable. Aduke, it is good to see you, although in what appears to be a sorry circumstance. Please tell me your story; take your time and go at your own pace. I promise not to interrupt you except when necessary."

"Oh Tola, pardon me, Mother Olga Mary, you are a very busy person, would you have the time now to listen to a long, dreary and wicked story. The story of a once normal girl who chose to be wicked and selfish and got herself entangled with the devil; as was to be expected she got herself landed in a big mess."

"Please Aduke no self-pity. Tell your story unvarnished and the merciful Father will show us a way out of what you called a mess."

Aduke gives a deep sigh. "I am sure you will remember the handsome Ladi with the captivating smile whom I fell hopelessly in love with when we were in the third form," recalls Aduke falteringly with a wistful look.

"How could I or any of us forget him? Did we not spend days plotting how we could lure him into the net of the irrepressible Aduke," answers Mother Olga Mary. "When I told you all at the time that I no longer cared for him," Aduke continues, "it was a great lie. I was burning for him. I was literally on fire. I have never loved like that before or ever since; indeed, I had never been in love until then. All day I would think about him. I would dream about him all night. At night, every night all my dreams were of him. I have come to realise that love is like fire. When fire is lit for a good purpose and when it is carefully and patiently tended, its controlled flame gives light and warmth; but when allowed to grow wild, the fire gets out of hand. It causes a lot of harm, destroying everything in its path. I became possessed. Ladi permeated my very life and existence. I lived and breathed for him. I did all I could to entice him. He did not even notice me. He was wrapped up in his love and admiration for Temilade. In my disappointment and anguish I swore to do everything within my power to spoil their relationship.

"Then one cool evening I was at the dancing school when Florence ran in – you remember Florence, the little imp. She was a year behind us. She was my messenger of sorts. I was on the floor with the chief instructor, Mr. B., who was showing me how to execute the 'Cuban Top' - and there was Florence frantically waving and gesticulating. She was making faces and hopping up and down. Fortunately Mr. B. had his back towards her. I thought that whatever news Florence was trying to convey to me must be important and urgent. I asked Mr. B. to be excused and quickly followed Florence towards the toilets..but instead of entering the ladies Florence made for the snack bar. Flopping onto a chair she signalled to me to take a seat. I had hardly sat down when she said, 'Guess what?'

"I retorted that I was not interested in taking part in any guessing game, adding, 'If you have news please let's have it. Can't you see that I am dying of anxiety?' 'Ladi and Temi got married this morning,' she finally blurted out. 'What sort of silly joke is that?" I asked.

"Before she could answer I added, 'Why did we not know they were going to be married? Someone who was invited would at least have told us.'

" 'I was told that they got married by special licence at the Central Registry,' said Florence. 'How can you be so sure?' I asked. 'Deji, my elder brother works at the Registry. He saw them and watched the ceremony from the window.' A great silence ensued. Florence then said, 'Aduke, say something.' I did not utter a word. 'Come on,' said Florence again.

"When there was no reply she looked sideways to see what was happening. It was at that precise moment that I was slumping down. In a flash Florence rushed to break the fall by catching me with both hands. In the process both of us crashed against the wall. Florence was breathing heavily. My head was cupped in her arms. Florence said I looked grey. My eyes dilated. I became perfectly still and made no sound at all. Though terribly alarmed, Florence had the presence of mind to let me down gently onto the bare floor. She dashed frantically into the ladies' room and came out with water and sprinkled it over me. After a few minutes I coughed; then I sneezed. Florence now bent over me gently, wiping my face and arms. She then sat on the hard floor placing my head on her lap and yelled for the snack bar attendant. Between both of them I was gently laid on the couch in the bar. 'What happened?' asked the attendant. 'She slipped and fell, hitting her head against the pillar. Her thick braided hair cushioned the blow,' Florence answered promptly. 'She is much better now. I'll get a taxi and take her home.'

"Then Mr. B. came into the bar. 'What happened?' he too asked. 'I was all the while waiting for her on the dancing floor.' When Mr. B. heard Florence's account he became understandably worried. 'Shall we take her to the hospital?' he asked. At this point I said almost inaudibly that I was fine and would prefer to go home. Mr. B. then drove us both to our house. Fortunately nobody was at home. Florence piloted me into my bedroom. We both sat down, not saying a word. It was Florence who broke the silence. 'The marriage has put a stop to it all. You can now settle down and get yourself another boyfriend'. 'No way!' I shouted hoarsely: 'Temi has won this particular battle but the war continues.' 'What do you want to do? What can you do?' asked Florence. 'A lot,' I snapped. 'I shall give them a fight. I shall give them hell. I even offered to be his concubine but he spurned me. He will pay.' 'Just be careful,' whispered Florence. On this note she quietly left to go home."

Aduke continues: "I had almost perfected my plans when I learnt Ladi had left for London. Later Temi went to join him. I then decided to pursue them. In the meantime I had requested a cousin employed at the Student Affairs Section in London to find out for me Ladi's residential address, which he did. I got to London two months after Temi's arrival. I got there just in the nick of time. Ladi wanted to take a lease on a super flat in Golders Green. He was just about to pay the rent. Zacc, my boyfriend then, who was besotted with me, was in charge of the letting agency. At my prompting he aborted the lease. Ladi and Temi were very disappointed.

"I did all sorts of things to make them uncomfortable. On their return to Nigeria I planted a steward in their home. He caused them a lot of distress. In the end he was sacked. I planted a sweet young lady in Ladi's office, employed as his secretary. I had previously primed her. She was to seduce Ladi with a view to wrecking their marriage; but it did not work. The bond of love between Ladi and Temi was really strong and extraordinary. It was brought home to me what a strong, binding tie true love could be. The poor girl returned to Europe badly bruised and with a broken heart; she had in the process fallen in love with Ladi. "I tried all sorts of tricks but to no avail. I became frustrated and angry. I cursed my lot. I fumed. I raved. I became completely exhausted and tired of living."

At this point Mother Olga Mary asks Aduke to pause for a while and calls for refreshments. Aduke then continues unburdening her heart, disclosing to Mother Olga Mary that she eventually got married and that it was a loveless union arranged to pacify her mother. "I was rescued by fate from the unwanted marriage," explained Aduke, "as my husband, who was fifteen years older than me, died. Fortunately, he left me his fortune. We had produced a son. I did not get on with my son or his wife. My churlish behaviour towards them drove them away from Nigeria.

"I was then left high and dry. I got fed up with

myself in spite of my wealth. I did not know where to turn. Out of boredom and loneliness I went in search of my son and his family. I eventually caught up with them in Cape Town. I was horrified to discover that my granddaughter had been gravely ill. I was told that her life was saved by the timely assistance of a Nigerian couple. I was shattered and mortified when I found out the identity of the persons involved. Would you believe, Mother Mary, that my family's benefactors were none other than Ladi and Temi? I became thoroughly ashamed. I came to the conclusion that fate was not quite finished with me. I was filled with remorse. I became truly penitent and, as a result, I went to my priest who sent me to you. So here I am seeking ways to atone for my many sins and wickedness." At this juncture Aduke bursts out in tears, weeping like a child, her chest heaving as she sobs her heart out. Bitter tears roll down her cheeks.

Mother Olga Mary allows her to cry to her heart's content. After some time, Mother Olga Mary holds her in her arms just as she had done in the old days, consoling her. She prays for her, asking God to grant her inner peace and time to make atonement for her sins. Aduke then calms down. She asks Mother Olga

Mary how much it costs to maintain the school each year. She wants to be allowed to contribute a substantial sum towards it. But Mother Olga Mary informs her that the existing sponsors are wealthy and may not wish to have any assistance. When she insists that Mother Olga Mary introduce her to the benefactors to see if some arrangement could be made for her to contribute, she returns home much relieved and in a far better frame of mind.

A few days later Mother Olga Mary contacts Aduke to confirm that the two benefactors have agreed to see her the following day to discuss the matter. Aduke arrives in good time and as they are discussing the good old days, the two benefactors arrive. Aduke is completely astounded to discover that they were none other than Ladi and Temi.

There is no problem in reaching an understanding as to how Aduke could help finance the girls' home as well as her role in the running of the home. It was agreed that she would be Mother Olga Mary's assistant in running the home. A second similar home was to be established in a town twenty miles away. The financing of the new project would be borne equally by Ladi and Temi on the one hand and by Aduke on the other. The arrangement would work perfectly well.

Aduke becomes a conscientious worker within the home. The young girls benefit tremendously from Aduke's contributions both in her teaching and financial support. She always defers to Mother Olga Mary as the head of the institution and in the process Aduke becomes humbler, wiser and more approachable. She never ceases to amaze and impress both Mother Olga Mary and Father Anthony, her priest. Her relationship with Ladi and Temi has changed completely and unbelievably. They are like a brother and sisters.

In due course with the help of her solicitor Aduke sets up a trust fund for all her charitable works. She becomes more of a worker within the church rather than the socialite she was before. She becomes known for her good works and kind deeds. The complete change in her is really impressive. She has been transformed into a totally different person. Mother Olga Mary is so impressed with the changed Aduke, so much that she wishes to show her off to the three other members of their group, Tolu, Teju and Ronke. She goes to a great length to trace them. They are invited to attend a surprise party that the home is hosting to honour Aduke's birthday.

On the day, Aduke is ushered into the room where her former classmates are already seated. They are all pleased to see Aduke and impressed to learn of Aduke's philanthropic work which has been widely publicised. They are amazed that the frivolous and mischievous Aduke has metamorphosed into such a generous spirit. On the following day they have lunch together. They reminisce about old school days and discuss what they have been doing since they parted. Ronke was a secretary; now retired, she offers to assist at the girl's home, two days a week. Teju, a medical doctor, offers free medical services. Tolu, who is a full time housewife, offers to teach homecraft.

Now that the relationship between Aduke and her son and his wife has improved, both of them return home to Nigeria. Thus Aduke has the privilege of enjoying her old age surrounded by members of her family. When she dies she leaves half of all her possessions to a foundation that will continue to run all her charities. The remaining half is left to her son and other members of her family.

Three years after Aduke's death a new chapel built in her memory by her son at the girls' home is dedicated. Thus Aduke, the mischievous, irresponsible and irrepressible girl, the vengeful and wicked woman, died as a God-fearing and highly respected philanthropist. She had indeed atoned for all her sins. Even in death her work of atonement still continues.

YORUBA LOVE STORIES

Design Management: OsanNimu
Illustration: Phil Wrigglesworth
Graphic Design: Leo Cooper, Angela Lyons
Design Direction: Ayo Alaka
Printed in India by Imprint Digital Ltd.